Yes, they'd actually kissed!

"You're not going to tell me it was the drink doing the kissing."

"You were doing the kissing!"

"I did have help," Joel argued.

"Don't read too much into it."

Amber turned, to find him looming over her, his hands on either side trapping her against the counter. "A mild celebration," she said, fighting down panic, "in honor of your exhibition."

"Do you celebrate with all your artists this way?"

"Of course not!" For the life of her she couldn't think of anything more to say.

He smiled then. "Good," he said, and took his hands away, moving back from her. "I didn't think so."

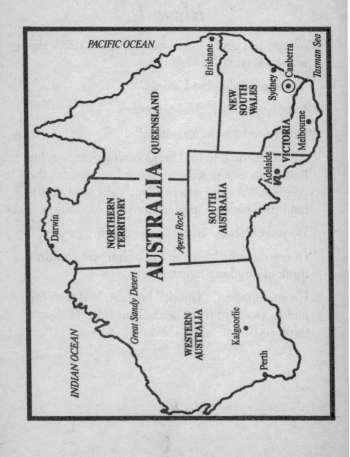

DAPHNE CLAIR

And Then Came Morning

Harlequin Books

TORONTO • NEW YORK • LONDON
AMSTERDAM • PARIS • SYDNEY • HAMBURG
STOCKHOLM • ATHENS • TOKYO • MILAN
MADRID • WARSAW • BUDAPEST • AUCKLAND

Harlequin Presents first edition September 1993
ISBN 0-373-11586-5

Original hardcover edition published in 1992
by Mills & Boon Limited

AND THEN CAME MORNING

CHAPTER ONE

NEW YORK was in the grip of a heatwave. A hot yellow sky oppressed the city, and the steady roar of traffic passing along the street was supplemented by hundreds of air-conditioning exhausts spilling warm used air out on to the pavement. Dodging one such blast as she passed a deli displaying lengths of salami and basketfuls of bagels, Amber nearly collided with a man going the opposite way, and narrowly missed stumbling off the kerb into the path of one of the city's thousands of yellow taxi cabs.

The man momentarily took her arm, steadying her.

'Thank you,' she said. 'Sorry.'

'Take care, now!' he admonished mildly, casting a fleeting and perhaps slightly critical glance at her high-heeled tan pumps, before going on his way.

New Yorkers, she thought, were like that. Busy and often in a hurry, and with the quality of self-confidence that others sometimes called brashness, yet they could take time to show concern for a stranger. She had lost count of the number of times well-meaning people, noticing her antipodean accent—although several had thought she was English—had told her to take care of herself, her baggage, her purse. But this was not her first visit, and, as on the other occasions, she had not experienced any particular problems.

She rather liked the city's hustling, bustling air, and even the heat was not intolerable. Summers back home could turn on sizzling temperatures, too.

All the same, it was a pleasant relief when she entered the artificially cool, still air of the Apple Gate Art Gallery. The doorway was modest, almost hidden, but inside was a roomy, marble-floored lobby, and the wide doors to the main gallery were open.

A couple of crates stood on the floor with some canvases stacked against them, and bits of packing were strewn on the floor near by. A man on a stepladder was adjusting a large unframed picture directly opposite the door. He wore a crumpled pale blue shirt and frayed jeans. His shoulders were very broad, and untidy, almost black hair covered his collar. One of Harry's assistants, presumably.

As she walked forward he turned his head, his hands still on the painting. 'The exhibition doesn't open until five,' he said, glancing indifferently at her. 'Come back in a couple of hours.'

'Harry's expecting me,' she said, advancing into the big room. The canvas was partly obscured by the man's body, but she could see the typically vibrant colour, leavened by sombre black and purple. It didn't seem to include the characteristic newspaper clippings that occurred so often in Matheson's work that they had become something of a trade mark.

There were other paintings on the walls, with their numbers beside them. Even a quick look made her want to study them more closely. They were good. But then she had known that Joel Matheson was good—a few examples of his work had found their way back to his native Australia, and she had seen prints and reviews in the art magazines she regularly ordered from America.

The man raised the corner of the painting a fraction and without looking at her asked, 'Is that straight?'

Amber checked with an expert eye. 'Yes.'

'Right.' He turned on the ladder and in one fluid movement leaped to the ground, shabby trainers cushioning the thud as he landed facing her. He was taller than she had expected, a big man altogether, and she had to quell an instinct to back off from him. His knees flexed, he flung up his head to flip a hank of hair out of his eyes, and then steadied himself and stood regarding her, his thumbs hooked into his belt.

Amber felt her hackles rise. His inspection was dispassionate rather than overtly sexual, but it was thorough all the same. His eyes were hazel, tending towards brown, and they took in her loose cream shirt and natural silk jacket and skirt and the businesslike leather bag hanging on her shoulder, then moved to her slender feet and ankles before returning to her face and the sleekly cropped, shining copper hair that framed it. She fancied that the look was faintly disparaging, and even that he had given a small, disapproving shake of his head before he said, 'Harry's expecting you?'

'He said any time after three.' Refraining from glancing at her watch, which showed precisely five minutes past the hour, she added, 'I'm Amber Wynyard. Perhaps you'd tell him I'm here?' Her voice was pleasant but firm. He was terribly good-looking in the slightly battered way that was supposed to set feminine hearts a-flutter, and obviously he knew it. At a guess there was nothing much between his ears except over-inflated male ego.

As the thought took shape in her mind, something in the man's eyes changed. She had an impression of unwelcome surprise, followed by amusement. 'Sure,' he drawled. Without moving from the place where he stood, he jerked his head to one side and called, 'Harry! A *lady* to see you!'

Not by a blink did she betray that she had noticed the emphasis. She gave him a dismissive nod and said, 'Thank you,' with only the merest hint of dryness. Then she deliberately half turned from him and stood waiting, until Harry Gates appeared in an insignificant doorway in a corner of the gallery, and hurried across the space between them to meet her as she started towards him. In contrast to his gallery assistant he was impeccably dressed, his suit, shirt and tie co-ordinated with faultless taste in shades of plum and grey.

'Amber!' He held out both his hands and clasped hers, bending his handsome, silver-dusted head to kiss her cheek. 'You look wonderful!'

'No, she doesn't.'

Amber reflexively turned to the man still standing behind her as Harry relinquished her hands.

'I beg your pardon?' she said in a frosty voice.

'You shouldn't wear that blah kind of colour.' She had been right about the disparaging look. Those almost brown eyes were definitely critical. 'It doesn't do a thing for you,' he added, sounding almost angry. 'Titian would have been wild about your hair.' He came closer, and he was so big that Amber again, with some difficulty, restrained herself from retreating before him. 'Old copper,' he said softly, his eyes narrowing in concentration. 'The kind that's been lovingly polished for years and years until it acquires that warmth of colour. But why have you cut it off?' he asked reprovingly.

'It's cool,' she answered, defensive even as she reminded herself it was not his concern. About to tell him so, she was stopped by Harry's deprecating laugh.

'Joel!' he protested. 'You mustn't say things like that to Amber. You've only just met—I take it you two *have* met?'

Amber wasn't really surprised. The sinking feeling in her stomach had told her even before Harry's casual use of the name that this rude, hulking slob was Joel Matheson, the man who painted with the touch of a dark angel.

Wincing inwardly, she said, 'Not formally,' and held out her hand, to have it enveloped in a firm but unexpectedly gentle clasp, considering the size of his. 'Mr Matheson didn't tell me who he was,' she added to Harry.

'Name's Joel.' He released her hand, giving her a quizzical look. 'Do you want me to call you Miss Wynyard?'

'No, of course not.' She tried to sound friendly, but her voice was stiff. Her body too, she realised, making a conscious effort to relax rigid muscles.

Harry shifted uneasily, and Joel glanced at him, his mouth quirking at one corner. 'Harry's afraid I've offended you,' he said, returning his gaze to her. He asked seriously, 'Are you offended?'

'I've been dealing with artists for years,' Amber replied.

He blinked and looked harder at her, his eyes searching the clear green depths of hers. 'You are,' he said. 'But it's true, you know. And a shame. You could be gorgeous.'

Refraining heroically from retorting that he could do with a shave and a clean-up himself, Amber said, 'I don't have any particular desire to be gorgeous, thank you.'

She was about to turn the conversation to something else when Joel asked, 'Why?'

The question threw her for a second. Then she said, 'I don't think that's a subject we should get into at the moment. I came to see your work.'

He looked as though he was about to argue the point, but Harry threw him a look that clearly conveyed 'Shut up', and said hastily, 'I asked Amber to come in early so she could get a good look before the mob arrives. But as you can see, Amber, we're still getting the paintings arranged. You don't mind if we talk later?'

With a hand on her arm, he steered her over to the wall near the main doors and thrust a catalogue into her hand. 'I know you prefer to look around quietly on your own. If you'll excuse us, we'll get the last few hung while you do that. Joel likes to do it himself—or at least have a major say in how it's done. Says at his first showing one of the works was hung sideways...'

Harry drifted off, and Amber slowly inspected the exhibition, trying to ignore the low-voiced conversation behind her. Usually it would have been easy, but there was something about the timbre of Joel Matheson's voice that impinged on her consciousness, though the words were hardly riveting... 'Up a bit, then? Is that it? OK, let's look at it. Mmm. Maybe the other one should be in that space, after all...'

Amber bent her concentration to the painting before her. At first glance it was deceptively pretty, a chocolate-box picture of a vase of varicoloured poppies, painted with bold, sure brush strokes. Two of the flowers were red. One had dropped a petal that lay disturbingly like a puddle of blood on a newspaper—an actual whole, folded newspaper glued to the canvas, its headline proclaiming more bomb deaths in...

The name of the country was folded under, but Amber didn't bother to lean close and squint at the smaller print. The message was clear and universal. It was a typical Matheson work, but like all his paintings had its own unique touch. His forte was taking the clichéd objects of everyday life and of 'pretty' art and juxtaposing them with images of anguish and violence, producing powerful statements which critics interpreted as political comments on society, on the problems of humanity, on the world as Matheson saw it, although the artist himself refused to talk about the meaning of his work.

Another picture was painted over a page of newspaper, a series of dramatic, intricately interwoven, slashing strokes of red and black resembling flowers on long stalks, through which the print showed a report of a flower show, a set of photographs of some society party, and an advertisement for a fashion house. Only when she was about to move past it did she discover that at a certain angle the black lines resembled bars and the red slashes a forest of despairing arms lifted behind them, the flowers and buds suddenly becoming spread fingers and clenched fists. She had to stop and look again.

The men were packing up, shoving paper into the crate, folding the ladder. She heard them leave when she was standing in front of the large canvas facing the door. The colour seemed layered across the top edge of the painting—poppies again, she guessed, although the painting was impressionistic, without the realistic detail of the still life on the other wall. Below the splashes of crimson, orange and pink was a band of green, again vaguely resembling flower stalks, that rapidly darkened towards the bottom of the frame into a confusion of black and dark reds and purples with smears of white. And there were bits of newspaper, not cuttings but small torn and crumpled scraps, and pieces of old sepia photographs there, some painted over, lying as though dropped on the ground. It was like a worm's eye view of a field strewn with rubbish.

'You're too close,' Joel Matheson said in her ear, almost making her jump. 'Move back.'

Obediently she walked across the floor, while he loped silently at her elbow. When she turned, the bright splashes at the top of the picture had become poppy flowers blowing in the wind, and the lines and whorls below resolved themselves into a shadowy, distorted jumble of half-buried skeletons, rusting weapons and decomposing limbs and faces, some with open mouths, reminding her of Edvard Munch's nightmarish work, *The Scream*. She felt her stomach cringe.

She glanced at the catalogue she was holding. The painting was called *Flanders*.

'Have you been to Europe?' she asked, trying to minimise the impact the painting had on her.

'Last year. My grandfather fought at Flanders in the First World War. He used to tell me about it sometimes, when I was a kid. The trenches, the mud, his mates being killed all around. His best friend was blown to bits beside him . . . he helped put the pieces in a sack. Now it's green grass and cornfields and poppies...but you feel as though you're walking over a graveyard.'

'It's good,' Amber said briskly. 'They're all good.'

'Thanks.' He looked down at her with a tinge of irony in his gaze, but she was studying the catalogue. 'You a special friend of Harry's?' he asked.

Amber looked up at the overt speculation she heard in his voice and said, 'Not special. We've known each other for quite a long time.'

'So how come you rate your own private preview? Are you a critic?'

'Didn't Harry tell you?' She had assumed Harry would mention her involvement to the artist. 'I have a gallery in Sydney,' she said, starting to explain.

'You're buying?' The interest in his eyes sharpened.

Before she could answer, Harry came out again, smoothing his tie with one hand, his hair with the other. 'You'd better get going, Joel,' he said.

'What?' Joel seemed puzzled.

Pained, Harry said, 'You're not going to appear at the opening like that, are you?'

Joel looked down at his attire with slight surprise. 'I'll change if you like,' he offered.

'I do like,' Harry told him. 'And so will your adoring public. Can you be back here in time?'

'Sure. I don't have to wear a tie, do I?'

Suppressing an obvious sigh, Harry said kindly, 'Not necessarily. I'll settle for a decent shirt and trousers. Ironed. And socks,' he added.

'Socks,' Joel echoed.

'And shoes. Clean. Not those grubby old sneakers.'

Amber thought she caught a gleam of amusement in Joel's eyes, but he said solemnly, 'Shoes. I'm not sure I have any.'

'Buy some!' Harry ordered.

'Buy shoes,' Joel repeated with the air of a child memorising a message. He sketched a mocking salute and turned to leave. With his hand on the outer door he swivelled his head to look back at Amber. 'You're staying for the formal opening?' he asked.

'Yes.' She hadn't had a chance to talk to him and Harry about the possibility of a showing in Sydney, and, besides, one never knew what useful contacts one might make over the hors-d'oeuvres and champagne at an opening.

Joel nodded. 'Good!' he said decisively, and went out.

Recognising with astonishment a ridiculous feeling of pleasure breaking through the annoyance he had aroused in her, Amber told herself that he wanted her to stay around to ensure her interest in his paintings. Which was fair enough, after all. Her only interest in him was as an artist—his personality had no appeal for her. Still . . . she turned back to the display on the gallery walls . . . he really was a genius at what he did.

'What do you think?' Harry asked her.

'Brilliant,' she answered. 'You were right. He may be a pretentious boor, but he knows what he's doing with a brush.'

'He's not so bad,' Harry protested mildly. 'A little unconventional, but what artist isn't?'

Amber shrugged. 'Anyway, the man can paint.'

'I haven't told him you're thinking of showing his stuff.'

'Oh?'

'Well, he can be a bit...difficult. I thought perhaps you should meet first. Get to know each other. See how you hit it off.'

'We didn't,' Amber said succinctly. 'But I still want to exhibit his work.'

'Of course I may sell all these...' Harry looked about.

'Have you ever sold everything from an exhibition, Harry?'

He looked sheepish.

'How fast can he work?' Amber asked.

'Ask him. I don't know.'

'The cream will go, I suppose,' Amber admitted. 'But if he can produce more to this standard...'

'He does have other work in his studio. This is only a selection.'

'Of the best.'

'That's a matter of opinion, of course.'

'Yes. Well, I'd like to see what else he has.'

'I'll try to talk him into it,' Harry promised.

'I should think he'd jump at the chance, surely?' Most artists in her experience would kill to have a gallery show their work.

Harry shook his head. 'He's a bit reticent, you know.'

'I know he doesn't give interviews. But he must talk to dealers.'

'Sometimes,' Harry said cautiously. 'But hardly anyone's allowed in his studio.'

The slob was a prima donna, Amber thought resignedly.

'But he seemed to like you.' Harry brightened.

'You could have fooled me,' Amber told him. 'Didn't you hear him on the subject of my appearance?'

'He's an artist.'

A feeble excuse, Amber considered, but didn't say so aloud. Harry was apparently prepared to condone most things on that ground. She herself would put up with a lot to secure a good exhibition. It didn't mean, however, that she had to profess a liking for Joel Matheson as a person.

People had begun to drift in and disperse themselves about the gallery before the painter returned. Amber, with her back to the door, was holding a narrow-stemmed glass and exchanging small talk with a youngish female journalist when the other woman's gaze slid interestedly past her shoulder and stayed there for several seconds.

'That's him, isn't it?' she said at last to Amber. 'Matheson.'

Amber turned her head obediently and confirmed, 'Yes, it is.'

It wasn't exactly a transformation, but there was certainly an improvement. His freshly ironed fawn shirt was open-necked and casual, teamed with a pair of darker jean-style trousers belted flamboyantly in tooled leather with a silver buckle, and his feet were respectably shod in brown leather loafers, showing a glimpse of bright yellow socks at which she mentally raised her brows. He had shaved too, and combed his hair, although to Amber's critical eye it was still too long. Altogether, though, she wasn't surprised at the gleam of feminine interest in her companion's eyes.

Joel caught her own eyes then, and she hastily looked away.

'He's coming over,' the other woman said. 'Do you know him?' Her voice held a trace of envy.

'We met this afternoon,' Amber admitted. She downed the rest of her drink, feeling a need to fortify herself.

A big hand slid into view to take the empty glass. 'Let me get you some more,' Joel offered.

'Thank you,' she muttered to his right shoulder.

The journalist said, 'You're the guest of honour, of course,' and eagerly introduced herself, holding out a long-fingered, elegant hand.

Joel took it in his free one and smiled down at the woman. 'Hi. Another drink for you too?'

'Oh, no. I've hardly started on this one. I'd love to talk with you, though.'

'Sure,' he agreed easily. 'Later, OK?' He smiled again, his eyes expressing a lazy appreciation as he slowly released the woman's hand. 'I'll catch up with you.' There was a wealth of promise in his voice.

Amber noted that he didn't seem to have any objections to the journalist's appearance. Quite the contrary, in fact.

Then she felt a compelling hand at her waist, and Joel was taking her with him across the room, saying, 'What were you drinking?'

'Champagne,' she said. 'Isn't everyone?'

'Some are on orange juice,' he replied. 'I'm glad you're not a teetotaller.'

'It's nice to think you approve of something about me.'

Ignoring the sarcasm in her voice, he said, 'I approve of a lot about you. I like your hair, and your voice, and those snappy green eyes. You've got nice legs—what I can see of them—and under that horrible suit I suspect there's a decent figure.'

'You can stop right there! Anyway,' she added, 'you *don't* like my hair. You said so.'

'I love the colour. Don't like the cut, but that's easily fixed. You can grow it.'

'I have no intention of growing it!' Amber said crossly. 'Not for you or any man!'

He stopped near the bar, and looked at her, his head cocked enquiringly. 'What have we done to you?'

He looked as though he was actually waiting for an answer. Exasperated, she said, 'Don't you know how to conduct a normal conversation?'

'What's abnormal about this one? I'm interested in you.'

Nonplussed, Amber stared up at him.

'Aren't you interested in me?' he asked her.

Amber found her voice. 'Only interested in your paintings,' she assured him tartly. Then she added, 'I thought you were going to get me a drink.'

He grinned and said, 'I am. Don't move.'

By the time he came back with two glasses in his hands, she had recovered her poise. 'About your work——' she began, her voice deliberately crisp.

'I never talk about my painting,' he interrupted.

'But I'm a dealer,' she explained. 'Not a journalist.'

'So what? You either like my stuff or you don't. You said it was good. I guess you like it.'

'I do like it. Very much. Most artists are only too glad to talk about what they're doing...'

He shook his head decisively. 'If I haven't conveyed all I want to say through my paintings, then what's the use of trying to explain them? That's the whole point of art.' He looked about impatiently. 'Why are there never enough places to sit down at these affairs? Do you want something to eat?' Without waiting for her reply, he signalled to one of the waiters threading through the rapidly increasing crowd. When the man thrust a tray of titbits before them, Joel cast her a glance that put her in mind of a large hound that had just brought in the morning paper for its master. 'Have some,' he invited.

Amber had very recently endured a long flight with airline meals served at odd hours. Her insulted digestion had not yet recovered. She looked at the tiny pastries adorned by unidentifiable tortured mounds of sickly-coloured mush, and her stomach recoiled. 'No, thanks.'

'Sure?' Joel insisted anxiously.

'Quite sure, thank you.' She smiled at the waiter to soften the firm reply. 'Maybe later.'

Joel shrugged and took a handful of the things himself before the waiter left. One went into his mouth and he apparently swallowed it whole. 'I haven't eaten since breakfast,' he explained, catching her gaze. 'Tell you what, let me take you out to dinner. Now, if you like.'

'You can't go anywhere now,' she protested. 'You've got to be here for at least another hour.'

He sighed. 'I suppose so.' He selected another bite-size pastry, this time chewing on it a couple of times before washing it down with champagne. Looking with faint surprise at the one remaining in his fingers, he said reflectively, 'These taste like cardboard and wet cotton wool. What do you s'pose that pink stuff is?'

'I hate to think,' Amber answered, averting her eyes from the slightly off-centre fluted spiral sitting on a round of pastry and topped with a dispirited slice of stuffed olive. 'Harry's probably spent a fortune on the catering.'

As if the sound of his name had summoned him from the ether, Harry appeared at her side. 'Joel,' he said, 'I want to introduce you to——'

'What is this, Harry?' Joel asked. He was regarding the savoury with a fascinated air, holding it up so that he could inspect it.

'I don't know,' Harry said. 'Roe, maybe.'

'Roe. Fish eggs?' Joel enquired, his eyes suddenly gleaming. He returned his gaze to the pastry, apparently absorbed. 'Fish eggs made to look like candy?'

'I guess so. Look, excuse us, Amber, won't you?' Harry plucked at Joel's arm. 'There's someone I want you to meet,' he reiterated.

'Oh, sure,' Joel answered obligingly. 'That waiter had a whole tray full of these,' he said, as though imparting vital information.

'Over here——' Harry persisted.

'Amber,' Joel said, as he made to obey the insistent pressure on his arm, 'keep this for me.'

Instinctively Amber held out her hand as he passed the thing to her and ambled off at Harry's side.

Keep it? What was she supposed to do? Nurse the damned thing for him all night? And what on earth did he propose to do with it? He'd said they tasted like cardboard and cotton wool, hadn't he? How long did he expect her to hold it? Wrathfully she regarded his retreating back, tempted to throw the repulsive object at it. That would create a stir. Give the reporters something to report on.

A waiter sidled by with an empty tray. 'Excuse me!' she said peremptorily, and, when he turned enquiringly, 'Mr Matheson wants this kept,' she told him, somewhat to his bemusement. Placing it in the centre of the crumb-flecked white doily on the tray, she said, 'Would you please put it in a safe place for him?'

The man was too well trained to suggest that either she or the guest of honour had lost their marbles. He said, 'I'll find a bag for it,' and serenely bore the tray with its sole occupant off to the nether regions where Harry allowed the caterers to prepare their miracles of culinary craft.

Five minutes later he returned with a small white paper bag carefully held, and she said, 'You might as well give it to Mr Matheson. He's over there.'

He was the centre of an admiring circle, including the woman journalist who had been talking to Amber earlier. His head bent attentively, he smiled at something the woman said. As the waiter approached the group, Amber stopped watching and turned to make her way through the crowd to the door. Although she seldom suffered much from jet lag, the long flight followed by the heat of the streets and the noisy chatter of the now packed gallery had begun to take their effect. Her head was starting to ache, and her stomach felt empty. She should not have allowed Joel to press the second glass of champagne on her either. It had made her queasy. She would contact Harry tomorrow and set up a private meeting with his protégé.

It was still hot in the street. She hailed a cab and, reaching the air-conditioned comfort of her hotel room, had room service send up a light meal and coffee. Then she stepped under a cool shower, and took an aspirin before climbing into bed. Outside it was not yet dark, and the traffic roared by unrelentingly, but she'd had a long day, with time changes along the way. Although she had slept after a fashion on the plane and had a short rest on her arrival, she felt very tired. She ought to be able to sleep.

It wasn't so easy, but after a time she dozed, not quite sleeping, alert to every footstep in the corridor and every squeal of brakes and distant siren from the streets. Then a light tapping on her door brought her fully awake.

'Who is it?' she called, sitting up. Someone probably had the wrong room, she thought crossly. Or it was the hotel staff checking something.

'Me. Let me in, Amber.'

Harry? He was the only one in New York who knew her hotel and room number.

Amber jumped out of the bed, hauling on the embroidered silk wrap she had bought in Singapore when she stopped over there on her last trip to Europe.

Outside night had fallen, but the traffic didn't seem to be any lighter.

Slightly muzzy, she opened the door without using the peephole provided for occupants to check their visitors, and fell back as she recognised the man standing there.

'Were you asleep?' Joel asked in astonishment as he stepped in and shut the door. 'It's early.'

'It may be early for you!' she snarled at him. 'I've been up since six o'clock Australian time. That's about thirty hours ago!'

'You flew in today? I didn't know that. I'm sorry!'

He looked so contrite that she softened a little. 'You weren't to know,' she mumbled, running a hand over her tousled hair. 'What do you want, anyway?' She didn't care if it sounded rude; he wasn't exactly into the niceties of good manners himself.

'I thought we had a dinner date.'

Amber said curtly, 'I never agreed to dinner or anything else.'

'You didn't say no.' He tried his smile on her. It was a fairly devastating smile; she had noticed that when he was talking to the journalist.

Amber remained unmoved. 'You take too much for granted,' she pointed out. Careful, an inner voice warned her. You want to get hold of this man's paintings. Don't antagonise him.

'I guess so,' he agreed humbly, but she didn't trust the glimmer she could see lurking in his eyes. 'Well, another time, maybe?' he asked hopefully.

'I want to talk to you, anyway,' she acknowledged. 'But not now.'

'No,' he agreed, and leaned closer, making her take a step back towards the bed. 'You look terrible,' he said earnestly.

'Thanks. That makes me feel a whole lot better.' She could do without having this man continually telling her how awful she looked.

He laughed. 'No, I mean you look tired. Get into bed.'

'I intend to—when you've gone.'

'Why not now?' he asked. 'I'll tuck you in.'

'You won't!' Her hands went to pull the edges of the gown close.

His mouth curved into an incredulous grin, even as she realised how foolish that had been. 'I won't rape you,' he promised kindly.

'I didn't think it for a minute!' she assured him with a touch of hysteria. 'Considering you've already made a habit of telling me how unattractive I am!'

'*Unattractive*?' He sounded almost outraged. 'I never said that!'

'Well, you certainly implied it!'

'No!' Vehemently he shook his head.

'You criticised my clothes, my hairstyle——'

'Because they don't do you justice!' he protested. 'I told you that. I must say I find the ruffled look quite fetching.' He regarded her hair with his head slightly tilted. Then his gaze shifted to the outline of her body in the tightly sashed jade silk and became frankly admiring. 'I like that, too,' he told her. 'It does things for that creamy complexion—and you *do* have a delectable figure.'

Infuriatingly, she felt her cheeks burning. 'Joel! Stop it!'

He looked almost hurt. 'Don't you like compliments? You know, you're very hard to please.'

'I would prefer you not to comment on my appearance at all!'

'Why?' As if struck by a sudden thought, he asked, 'Don't you like me?'

'I don't even know you!' Amber said. 'How do I know if I like you or not?'

'I like you,' he offered.

'I can't imagine why!'

'Why shouldn't I?'

'For one thing, I've been pretty sharp to you.'

'I guess you've just been yourself,' he suggested generously, if with some ambiguity. 'You could try being nice for a change.'

'Why?' she shot at him, trying some of his own tactic.

He considered. 'Harry says you want to show some of my paintings in Sydney.'

'Yes.' She closed her teeth on the word.

'What about lunch tomorrow?' he asked. 'You can practise.'

'Practise?'

'Being nice to me.'

'All right,' she said. 'Lunch tomorrow. You took the words right out of my mouth, actually.'

'Good. Now shall I tuck you in?'

'No.' She marched to the door and opened it. 'Goodnight, Joel.'

He sauntered over to her, and as he hovered, clearly contemplating a kiss, she glared up at him, daring him to try it. After a moment he smiled, shrugged, and as he passed her said, 'By the way, thanks for looking after my hors-d'oeuvre.'

'I hope you enjoyed it,' she said, very dry.

He looked at her with surprise. 'I didn't *eat* it!'

'Well, what on earth did you want it for, then?' she asked, realising even as she said the words what the answer would be.

'I thought you'd know,' he said, as though she were a slightly backward child. 'I'm going to paint it, of course.'

CHAPTER TWO

JOEL phoned Amber at ten the next morning. 'Do you like Middle Eastern food?'

'I don't know. I don't think I could cope with a highly spiced lunch today, though.'

'You're not sick, are you?'

'No. I just feel I ate too much yesterday, that's all.'

'You ate nothing at the opening.' He sounded slightly censorious.

'I had a meal here at the hotel.' Why was she making excuses to this man?

'A salad, I'll bet,' he said disgustedly.

'There's nothing wrong with a good nourishing salad.'

Joel snorted. 'I'll give you a decent meal.'

'I'm paying,' Amber hastened to claim.

'No, you're not. I invited you, remember?'

She counted to three. 'I was going to offer you lunch anyway.'

'Well, then, I beat you to it. This one's on me.'

Amber gave in gracefully.

He was wearing denims and a T-shirt, but at least they were clean, she noted, as he ran his eyes without comment over her buff-coloured skirt, white blouse and high-heeled sandals. She had guessed he would be wearing something casual, to say the least, and dressed herself accordingly.

The meal he and the waiter chose for her after consulting her general preferences turned out to be tasty but not over-spiced. She enjoyed it, and told Joel so over cups of strong, well-sweetened coffee.

'I knew you would,' he replied.

'You couldn't possibly——'

He leaned across the table, his chin on one big hand, regarding her intently. 'Why do you do that?'

'Do what?' Amber asked blankly.

'Keep backing off from me. Do I scare you?'

She knew she hadn't moved at all when he had suddenly loomed at her, but he was uncannily accurate about her inward shrinking. She said coldly, 'You're imagining things. I don't know what you're talking about.'

His steady gaze didn't waver, but a deep glint appeared in them. She felt her chin tilt infinitesimally in response. Their eyes locked in a moments-long, wordless challenge.

The waiter broke into the silence with, 'More coffee?' and Joel nodded.

Then he leaned back in his chair, arms folded, and as the man walked away said softly, 'Well?'

Amber had recovered her poise. 'I'd like to have a showing of your work in Sydney,' she said. 'Harry told me you have some paintings in your studio that were not included in his exhibition.'

'Yes.' His watchful expression didn't alter.

Mentally gritting her teeth, Amber went on, 'I'd like to see them.' It sounded abrupt, and she probably should have phrased it more tactfully. But she wasn't going to coax, pander to his ego. He could damn well take it or leave it. She would even be slightly relieved if he declined to co-operate.

His coffee steamed gently on the table in front of him, but he didn't move, just stared at Amber, apparently deep in thought. Then he said, 'All right. When?' and reached forward to take the cup and raise it to his mouth.

Surprised, Amber said, 'What about this afternoon?' Better, she thought, take advantage of the offer before he decided to retract.

'OK.' He drank some coffee, and put down the cup. 'Now?'

'Yes. If it suits you.'

Joel shrugged. 'I'm easy. You finished?'

Amber nodded, and Joel signalled the waiter for the bill.

He got them a taxi, and seated beside him she was uncomfortably conscious of his size, the length of his legs and the breadth of his shoulders. He sat with his knees parted and his loosely linked hands held between them. She found herself studying those hands that could wield a paintbrush with infinite delicacy as well as boldness, speculating on the latent strength of the long, blunt-ended fingers. His nails were short and clean, but she detected a faint line of blue paint on the quick of a couple of them.

Joel had been gazing out the window, but as if feeling her scrutiny he turned his head, and involuntarily she glanced up. He gave her a quirky smile that held a curious intimacy. Amber looked away.

They stopped at a brownstone building in Greenwich, and Joel said, 'It's a walk-up.'

The stairs were dark and creaked beneath their feet, but, when they reached the third floor and he unlocked a door and stood back for her to precede him, she walked into light.

The walls, where they were not hung with pictures, were the colour of sunshine, and there was a sunburst of a wool rug on the floor, set off by boards that had been sanded back to their natural colour and then coated with a clear, glossy finish. Through a pair of saloon-type doors Amber glimpsed a small kitchen. A wide archway framed a big bed covered with an Indian-print spread in dramatic shades of gold, with black designs. The cover was crooked, the pillows piled against the wall indented, and a rumpled shirt lay at the foot of the bed. A tall chest of drawers apparently wasn't large enough, for its top was piled with an assortment of clothing, books, pencils stuck in a coffee-mug, and other objects that baffled Amber's cursory glance.

In the living area a bean chair of dark gold velvet was humped in one corner, and a worn black leather couch with four squashed scarlet cushions had an open newspaper on it. Some pages had slipped to the floor. Two bentwood chairs flanked a small round table near the kitchen door, and a couple of antique chests seemed to serve for occasional tables. An overflowing bookcase ran along the outer wall under the two windows. Pieces of pottery sat on the top of it, mixed with old magazines, a couple of beer cans and a plate holding stale crumbs.

'Sorry,' Joel mumbled, and whisked the plate and the cans off to the kitchen, dumping them respectively in the sink and a rubbish bin in the cupboard underneath. There were other dishes already in the sink, Amber judged from the clatter he made when he added the plate to them.

She stepped over a magazine that was lying open on the floor, killing the urge to pick it up and find a place for it on the bookshelves. 'This isn't your studio?' she said.

'No. Here.' He came out of the kitchen and led her through a door into a small passageway. 'That's the bathroom,' he indicated as they passed another door. And this——' he opened another '—leads to the studio.'

It was a steep attic stair, and he gestured her to go first. At the top she walked into a large room lit by a skylight as well as arched windows that reached almost to the floor. An easel stood holding a canvas, and beside it was a table cluttered with tubes and brushes and stained rags. The smell of paint and linseed permeated the air, and unframed paintings leaned against the walls. A few had been framed and hung. At one end a huge series of shallow drawers occupied almost the entire wall, and there was a couch, shabby and rather uncomfortable-looking, shoved into a corner, crowding a full-length mirror on a stand. Swaths of cloth hung randomly over a nearby screen— green, pink, orange, kingfisher-blue, and a shimmering length of flame-coloured shot silk with a hint of purple in the folds.

'May I look?' Amber asked, walking towards the easel.

Joel shrugged, which she supposed constituted consent. He remained by the door, watching her. There was a tension in him, and she wondered if he regretted inviting her here.

She saw the silly little savoury from last night among the painter's paraphernalia on the table, and identified its twin on the canvas, larger than life-size, tipped at a rather drunken angle, the slice of olive precariously about to slide off. Behind it, sharing the

suggestion of an oval plate, lightly drawn, was a fish—
a very dead fish, slit for gutting, the job half done.
Even the spare pencil lines engendered a feeling of
revulsion.

Amber stepped back, taking a breath, and Joel said,
'Don't move!'

Startled, she looked at him. He was crossing the
floor to snatch up a sketch book and pencil from the
top of the bank of drawers, turning with narrowed
eyes to face her again.

'No!' Amber said, going towards him with a hand
outstretched as though to take the things from him.
'I'm not a model.'

'So what?' he demanded, throwing his hands apart
in exasperation, one still holding the pencil, the other
the sketch book. 'I hardly ever use professional
models.'

'I might have known you were a cheapskate.'

It came out without her thinking about it, a nasty
crack that she immediately regretted, even before she
saw the clamping of his mouth.

'So what's your price?' he asked her, and she almost
flinched at the dark, silky tone.

'I'm sorry!' she said. 'I didn't mean that.'

He gave her another of his oddly unsettling,
thoughtful looks, then said calmly, 'Apology accepted. Will you pose for me?'

'No.'

She thought his eyes were trying to bend her to his
will, then he dropped the sketch book carelessly
behind him and flipped the pencil on top of it. 'OK.'
He slanted a glance at her. 'Why? Most women would
jump at it.'

'I'm sure most would be terribly flattered. But not all of us are dying to be painted for posterity.'

'That doesn't answer my question.'

She looked at him squarely. 'For one thing, I don't have the time.'

After a moment he smiled. She knew he didn't believe that was the only reason, but before he could come back to it she said, 'I came to see your paintings.'

'Feel free,' he invited. 'Where shall we begin?'

An hour later Amber said, 'Yes, those five, for a start. What's in the drawers?'

'Mostly old stuff,' Joel answered dismissively. 'And some pastels I've been experimenting with.'

'Experimenting?' Amber's mental antennae came into play. When artists tried something they thought of as experimenting, the results were unpredictable: they could be a total botch, or something exciting. Often, because the medium or the style they were attempting was unfamiliar, the artists were the last to know if what they had done was any good. 'May I see?' she asked him.

She sounded imperious rather than pleading, and Joel's mouth curled as he looked down at her. 'Ask me nicely,' he taunted.

'I just did.' Irrelevantly, Amber wished he weren't so tall. It was a disadvantage, having to look up at him. She succumbed to a surprisingly urgent desire to wipe the smile off his face. 'You don't have to be afraid,' she said with devastating kindness. 'I expect they're quite good, really. And,' she added, digging in the rapier, 'you can't expect a dealer to make a decision on what works to show if she hasn't seen everything that's available.'

His face stony, Joel said, 'They're not available.'

He was going to call her bluff, she realised. She kept her voice level. 'I see. I'd like to look at them, all the same.'

Joel uttered a short word under his breath. 'Is that the best you can do?' he demanded witheringly.

Amber said tartly, 'What do you want—that I go down on my knees?'

'What I want...' he said, and allowed the silence to hang in the air. Meeting his eyes, hers widened, and Joel said softly, 'Yes. Why are you surprised?'

She'd been propositioned before, for heaven's sake. There was no reason for her to flush so wildly, for the blood to be beating a tiny tattoo in the veins at her temples, for her palms to be moist. She said cuttingly, 'I'm an art dealer.'

'You're a woman.'

'That has nothing to do with it.' She stopped, clenching her teeth at his sudden laughter.

'Why do you think I invited you here?' he demanded.

Her eyes sparked. 'I assumed it was because you wanted to see your work shown in your home country. It didn't occur to me that you were hoping for some more immediate form of gratification. Stupid of me not to have guessed that you're one of those ageing adolescents forever pursuing some fantasy of being the Great Lover, trying it on with every halfway pretty female who crossed your path. I should have recognised the type.'

'I'm not a type!'

Her mouth took on a sardonic curve. 'No?' she said with freezing disbelief.

'And I wasn't making a pass at you!' he said furiously.

Amber raised her brows in a gesture of extreme scepticism.

'And you're certainly not even halfway *pretty*!' he added, with positive savagery.

A chauvinist scorned! Amber thought. 'You're breaking my heart!' she mocked. 'I don't have any illusions about my looks, thanks.' She knew she wasn't ugly, but apart from her hair, which often drew second glances, there wasn't anything special about her.

'Huh!' Joel snorted impatiently. 'You have no idea!'

'What are you talking about?' Amber enquired, and then, 'What are you doing?'

For he was prowling round her, scowling and inspecting her with hard, intent eyes.

'Colour!' he said. 'You need colour.' He looked about, and hauled a couple of pieces of fabric from the screen in the corner. Before she could stop him he had thrown a piece of pink stuff over one shoulder and a vivid green swath across the other before stepping back.

'Better,' he said judiciously, before Amber found her voice and her hands scrabbled the material away from her.

'This is ridiculous,' she said. 'Joel ...'

But he wasn't listening. With an air of inspiration, he had grabbed the length of flame silk.

'Joel, don't ...'

Ignoring her attempt to ward him off, he draped it swiftly so that part of it framed her face, forming a loose cowl, and the ends were crossed at her throat and falling back over her shoulders. He took her protesting hands in his and looked at her, then pulled her unwillingly to the mirror.

'And anyway,' Amber was saying, 'redheads can't...'

'Look,' Joel ordered.

She was already looking. Disbelieving. This wasn't her, this mysterious, vital creature with the faintest hint of apricot in her complexion, jewel eyes and a delicate flush in her cheeks, and a parted, passionate mouth, as soft as rose-petals.

Hastily she closed it, but her eyes were reluctant to leave the vision in the mirror. It's illusion, she thought dazedly. I don't look like that. I could never look like that...

'You see?' Joel was saying in triumph. 'You have something far more exciting than prettiness.'

Exciting. The word made her heart give a quick thud of apprehension. Joel was standing just behind her now, and their eyes met in the mirror. She saw his darken, and then his hands were on her waist, he was turning her to face him...

'No,' Amber said. She was not struggling, but she held herself rigid, not looking at him.

'No?' His voice was a murmur, and his hands tightened.

She shook her head, her fingers going to prise his away from her waist.

Reluctantly he let her go, and the silk whispered down her hair, her back, and, as she moved her arms, slid to the floor.

She felt curiously naked. When she dared to look at Joel he was studying her with a strange, concentrated air.

'This is silly,' she said, trying to break the spell that seemed to hold her. 'I'm not a doll—or a model—for you to dress up, Joel. And I didn't come here to play games.'

'*Games*?'

She ignored the anger in his voice and rushed on. 'I would like to see the rest of your work, and particularly the pastels, but if you don't feel you want to show them to me...' Her shoulders lifted in a shrug. Let him fill in the rest as he chose. He could construe it as a willingness to compromise, or a flat refusal.

For a moment he just stared at her, then he swung away. 'All right,' he said, hauling open the top two drawers. 'Help yourself. Go on.'

She approached them slowly, as he stood there, and he gave a short laugh and said, 'I won't bite.'

He folded his arms and stood gazing remotely across the room at the windows while she carefully lifted the drawings and inspected them.

'When you said they were experimental,' she said some time later, 'I thought...'

'I know.' He glanced at her almost indifferently, but she caught a hint of—what?—*embarrassment* behind the indifference.

'Of course, we'd be taking a risk, showing them,' she said.

He looked at her properly then. 'Yes.'

'They're so different from your other work.'

Joel nodded.

'I want to do it,' Amber said.

She thought he almost smiled then. But all he said was, on a faint sigh, 'OK.'

'Pastels?' Harry queried the following afternoon, when Amber was at the gallery again. 'Joel's working in pastels?'

'Some,' Amber qualified. 'They're good.'

'Of course they would be. Everything he does is good.' Harry, perched on the edge of his desk while Amber occupied the visitor's chair, shifted a pen beside him and aligned it with another that lay on his immaculate blotter. 'So you managed to wheedle him into taking you to the studio.'

'I didn't wheedle! I asked and he said yes.'

Harry cast her a look of deep puzzlement, which quickly cleared. 'Of course, you're a woman and——'

'Now you stop right there!' Amber said. 'I'm a dealer just like you, and I didn't use any so-called feminine wiles on your golden boy...'

Harry held up a hand. 'Sorry. I just thought he rather fancied you, that's all. Well, you must admit it would give you an edge.'

'If it were true, maybe,' Amber admitted. She supposed Joel did fancy her in an odd way, if only because he wanted to make her over. A kind of Galatea to his Pygmalion.

Harry was studying her thoughtfully. 'I quite fancy you myself, as a matter of fact.'

Amber gaped a little, and he chuckled. 'Is it so strange? We've known each other a number of years now, and you're a very attractive young woman, in your own quiet, understated way. Of course, I'm years older, but not exactly doddering yet.' He smiled wryly. 'Not too old to appreciate your charms, anyway.'

'Of course you're not old,' Amber said. He was probably in his early fifties, and well-preserved at that. She had seen him squiring various quite glamorous ladies, but had never thought of him in a romantic way herself.

'Don't look so nervous,' he said. 'I'm not about to leap on you. I just . . . wanted you to know.'

'I'm . . . flattered,' Amber managed.

His eyes crinkled. 'But not thrilled.'

'Well, I never expected . . .'

Harry looked rueful. 'You know, I've got a little tired of being treated like a favourite uncle.'

'Sorry!' Amber said faintly. She looked at him carefully, trying to picture him in a different light from the one in which she had always regarded him—a knowledgeable, generous friend who had helped her in her chosen profession and with whom she had a pleasant, undemanding relationship, both professional and personal.

'Do you mind,' Harry said, as if he knew what she was doing, 'if I try to erase the image?'

He bent and took her hands, drawing her unresistingly to her feet. She wasn't nervous of him, just curious and a little hopeful.

He folded her expertly into his arms and said, smiling down at her lifted face, 'Perhaps I should tell you that my intentions are strictly honourable.'

Then he kissed her with that same expertise, taking his time and not forcing anything. It was very pleasant and after a while she placed her hands on his shoulders and held them as she kissed him back.

The quick tattoo of fingers on the door was followed by its opening immediately afterwards, and Amber pushed against Harry's chest, but he released her only slowly, as he looked up to see who it was.

'Hello, Joel,' he said easily.

Joel stood in the doorway, wearing a peculiarly blank expression. 'Sorry,' he said tersely. 'You did say three o'clock.' He hadn't looked at Amber at all.

Amber stood aside awkwardly as Harry said, 'Yes, I did.' Consulting his watch with an air of pleased surprise, he added, 'And you're on time.'

Amber said, 'Excuse me. I'll see you later, Harry.'

'I'll phone you,' he promised, smiling at her, and put a light hand on her waist as she walked the few steps to the door. Joel was blocking it. He stood aside, and for a moment his eyes brushed hers—only for a moment, but when Harry had quietly closed the door behind her she stood and took a deep breath to steady herself. Because Joel's quick, probing glance had seared.

It wasn't anything to do with him, she told herself, and there was certainly no earthly reason why she should feel guilty. Some embarrassment was understandable, but this ridiculous sensation of being caught out in something shameful—well, if Joel didn't like it, that was just too bad.

Harry took her out to dinner, amid discreet lights and potted palms. He wore a dinner-jacket and she wore silk in autumn colours. They talked like the old friends that they were, and laughed softly at shared jokes and discussed Joel Matheson's work.

'They're selling very well,' Harry told her about the pictures he was showing in the gallery. 'There won't be a lot left from there to take to Australia, I'm afraid.'

'You needn't try to sound broken-hearted,' she teased him. 'I know you're as pleased as Punch. And I don't blame you,' she added generously. 'I did notice a number of red stickers this afternoon.'

She pushed the memory of the incident in his office away from her, and allowed Harry to refill her wine glass.

'What about the pastels?' he asked idly, toasting her with his eyes.

'They're different,' Amber said.

'You told me that this afternoon. Only you didn't get around to telling me in what way. I guess we got ... side-tracked.'

Amber avoided his glance. She hadn't had time yet to think through all the implications of what had happened. 'Some critics may call them sentimental,' she said.

'Sentimental?' Harry put down his glass. '*Joel Matheson*? Sentimental?'

'Well, they're ... childhood memories, I should think,' Amber explained. 'Full of nostalgia—children playing among gum trees, an Aboriginal father with his family, lovers walking by a stream, landscapes with figures ... memories of home.'

'He's been living in the States for—what? Nearly twenty years,' Harry said.

'Fifteen, I believe,' Amber corrected. 'He came here when he was in his early twenties. He's always been thought of as a New York painter in spite of his Australian background, I know. But it's there inside him.'

'Well, some critics claim to detect a connection of course, but I've never seen it myself...'

'You would in these pastels,' Amber assured him. 'Even the colours are Australian—ochres and earthy reds, and the soft green of eucalyptus, and the brassy sunlight. Not a northern sun at all.'

'Well, well. They're not old work that he did when he first left Australia?'

'Oh, no. They have the hallmarks of maturity, the sureness of style. Besides, he said he'd done them recently. Experimental, he called them.'

Harry shook his head. 'Well, I'd never have believed it. *Are* they sentimental?' he asked her shrewdly.

Amber answered obliquely. 'They're not as fierce as his other work. But they have vigour and dash, and a kind of haunted quality.'

'Haunting?'

'No. Haunted,' Amber corrected firmly. 'By something coming from inside the artist himself. And he's achieved an amazing concept of the harsher aspects of the Australian landscape. In a superrealist style. The details are so finely rendered, they almost hurt.'

'Hmm.' Harry forked into his smoked salmon. 'Is he going to fly to Sydney for the exhibition?'

'I . . . haven't asked him yet.'

She always did try to persuade her artists to attend. Those who lived in Australia usually did, of course. Her occasional American exhibitors usually took the chance of combining business with a pleasant trip to another part of the world, but one or two had pleaded other commitments and Amber—and her patrons— had to be content with the paintings alone.

'If he's homesick,' Harry said philosophically, 'he'll jump at the chance.'

'Yes,' Amber agreed, experiencing a strange mixture of hope and trepidation. 'I suppose he might.'

CHAPTER THREE

BUT for the next few days Joel Matheson was strangely elusive. Amber had other contacts to see, and she spent some fruitful hours meeting people and exchanging information and ideas, but several times she phoned the number Harry had given her for Joel's home, only to receive no reply.

She checked the number in the telephone book, tried again, then called Harry to ask if he knew where Joel was.

'Haven't seen him,' Harry answered cheerfully. 'Gone to ground, has he?'

'Apparently. Where would he go?'

'No idea. He's probably holed up in his studio and not answering the phone.'

'How does he expect me to mount an exhibition for him if he's not available?' Amber asked, exasperated.

'Artists . . .' Harry said philosophically.

'Artists have to live in the real world like the rest of us,' Amber reminded him. 'I'm not surprised they used to starve in their garrets, if this is the way they carried on.'

Harry chuckled. 'Perhaps he's playing hard to get.'

'If he is, he's a fool! There are plenty of others out there clamouring for someone to hang their work in a gallery.'

'If he turns up here I'll tell him you've been trying to get in touch,' Harry promised. 'Are you busy tonight? Can I take you out to dinner?'

There was no reason why not, and after the briefest hesitation she accepted. She had scarcely had time to think about Harry's revelation of his feelings towards her, and she wasn't really taking it very seriously. He must have been in a sentimental mood, she decided. Or between girlfriends. She decided to be very brisk, and dressed in a black, slim-fitting dress that left her shoulders bare but otherwise covered her to the throat. When she surveyed her reflection in the mirror she had doubts, but it was too hot to wear anything with sleeves. Anyway, she had long ago learned to severely limit her travel wardrobe, and there wasn't a lot of choice.

Harry looked approving when he met her in the hotel lobby, and there was a new warmth in his eyes that made her heart sink. She greeted him with cool affection and tried to set the tone of the evening from there, relieved that he seemed content to have it so.

After their dinner, though, he asked if she would like to move on to a nightclub, and was obviously disappointed when she declined, pleading the need for an early night.

That was when he reached across the table and took her hand in his. 'Come back to my place for a nightcap, then?' he asked.

Amber instinctively tried to withdraw her hand, her back stiffening.

Harry laughed at her softly. 'Amber!' he chided. 'I'm not suggesting you stay the night. Do you think I've been blind to the subtle hints you've been throwing my way all evening?' He released her hand and sat back. 'We're old friends, aren't we? All I want is a little private time with you. I won't keep you late, I promise. And I won't try to lure you into my bed.'

'All right,' she said. She believed him. Harry was much too civilised to try crude macho tactics. And it wouldn't be the first time she had been to his apartment.

His home was a symphony of good taste, the big lounge all silver-grey and black warmed with touches of burgundy and rich blue. A picture window overlooked the city, and when she had admired his latest acquisitions—a small modern print and a rather large stainless steel sculpture—they sat companionably sipping warmed brandy and admiring the night view.

'Nice.' Amber settled back contentedly in the big leather armchair.

'Even nicer with you here,' Harry answered.

She gave him a restrained smile and lifted the balloon glass to her lips.

'Do you have a fella back home?' Harry asked.

Amber debated taking the easy way out, but she had never been good at lying, and anyway had found it always led to complications. 'No.'

'You've never been married, have you?'

Amber shook her head. 'Never.'

'I have. Broke up years ago. She's married to someone else now. They've got three kids.'

Regarding him curiously, Amber asked him, 'Do you want a family, Harry?'

'I'm too old for that now. Sometimes ... but no. I can't see myself as a father, can you?'

'Perhaps I don't know you all that well.'

He smiled. 'What about you? Do you want to settle down, have a husband and children?'

'No.' Amber shook her head. 'I've never wanted that.'

'Never?' Harry's brows rose.

Wordlessly, Amber shook her head again, and turned her gaze from him to look at the winking lights outside. It wasn't quite true, of course. Teenage dreams didn't count.

'Would you settle for just the husband, then?' he asked. 'There are some things about being married that I miss. Someone to unwind with, share silly little jokes with . . . just sit with sometimes, like this. I'm middle-aged, Amber. I'm getting too old for affairs.'

Amber wondered if she was supposed to sympathise. But he suddenly laughed again. 'I'm not making much of a job of this, am I? Forget my maunderings. It must be the brandy talking—and the wine I drank at dinner. You're an attractive young woman, and why should you be interested in a used-up old stick like me? Drink up, and I'll take you home.'

Amber looked at him, and laughed in her turn. 'If you're trying to make me feel sorry for you, Harry, it won't work. You're a handsome, intelligent, successful man in the prime of life, as if you didn't know it, and any woman would be flattered and delighted to be the object of your attentions.'

'Any woman?' Harry cocked his head. 'Including you?'

Trapped, Amber said, 'Well, of course I'm flattered . . .'

'But delighted is carrying it a bit far.'

Amber said, 'I'm different from most women——' Harry gave her an expressive, enquiring look, and she said hastily, 'No, I don't mean in that way. But I'm not interested in a relationship—of any sort.'

'Have you tried it?'

'A long time ago. I've a career, a business to run. It takes all my time, my energy. There isn't room for anything else.'

Shaking his head, Harry said, 'That's no way to live, Amber.'

'It suits me.' She finished the liquid in her glass and stood up. 'It's my way. Thank you for this evening, Harry. It's been nice.'

He made a rueful face. 'Nice for me too. But I'd hoped for...'

'I'm sorry,' Amber said.

'I won't take it as final,' he promised, stirring unease in her again. 'You didn't object when I kissed you the other day. If I've given you the impression that I'm looking for some sort of bloodless companionship, you couldn't be more wrong, you know.'

She wasn't sure how he came to have her in his arms. Obviously he'd had a lot of practice. She put protesting hands against his chest, but he took no notice of that, and she found her head tipped back against his cradling arm while he pressed a long, expert kiss on her lips.

This time she didn't make the mistake of responding, but just waited passively, surprised at the stirring of an urge to return the kiss. There was nothing threatening about it, only a pleasant insistence, but at last he released her with a smile. 'Forgive me?' he murmured.

'This time,' Amber said steadily. 'Just don't make a habit of it. Can you call me a cab, please?'

'I'll take you.'

'No. I'd rather take a cab.'

Harry shrugged. 'OK.' He cast her a slightly baffled look. 'I don't think you're as cool as you pretend, though.'

She met his eyes, deliberately. 'Give it up, Harry. I told you, I'm not like other women.'

He made a derisive little sound. 'If you're trying to say you're frigid, I don't believe it. Did someone tell you that?'

Amber shook her head. 'Harry, I want to go back to my hotel. This conversation is closed.'

She didn't, in the end, go straight back, though. About halfway there she realised that the cab was passing the brownstone building where Joel Matheson lived. His windows below the top floor studio were yellow with light. On impulse, she called to the cab driver to stop.

'I've changed my mind,' she said. 'I'm getting out here.'

When he had driven off, she stood on the pavement and wondered if she was crazy. The man might even have company. It was late.

Not that late, she reminded herself, glancing at her watch. Not, she was sure, late for Joel Matheson. Anyway, he had disturbed her in her hotel room after she had gone to bed. It wouldn't hurt him if she returned the compliment. If she didn't get hold of him now, she'd be lucky if she managed to see him again before she had to fly back home. The chance was too good to miss.

When he opened the door she wondered if he had been asleep. He looked bleary-eyed, but he was dressed in faded jeans and a paint-stained shirt which hung open and loose. He had acquired a dark growth of beard again, and his hair looked as though it hadn't been combed in days.

'How did you know?' he said, stepping back to let her in.

She walked past him, catching the smell of oil paints and sweat from his body, and of beer from a can that he was holding in one hand. 'Know what?'

Then, supposing he meant how had she known he was home, she opened her mouth to explain, but he said, 'That I'd finished.'

'Finished?'

He shut the door and turned again to face her blank stare. He said, 'That wasn't it?'

Amber shook her head. 'Shall we start again?' she suggested patiently.

He ran a hand through his hair and rubbed the back of his neck. 'Yeah, sure,' he said. 'Why don't you sit down?'

'Thank you.' She moved a couple of magazines from the sofa and looked about for somewhere to put them.

'Here.' Joel took them and dropped them on the floor, then swept a few more off and sat down himself, staring as though he didn't quite believe she was really there. She wondered how much he had drunk recently. A covert survey of the room showed her no more beer cans, although it was, if anything, more cluttered and untidy than the first time she had been there.

Joel made to raise the can in his hand to his lips, then said, 'Oh, sorry. Can I get you something? A drink? Coffee?'

Amber shook her head. 'No, thank you.' Politely she added, 'Don't let me stop you.'

Her glance at the beer might have been a little wary, though, because Joel grinned faintly and said, 'It's the first I've had in days. Honest.'

Looking at him carefully, she realised that if he wasn't drunk or hungover he was obviously bone-weary. Remembering what he had said at the door, she asked, 'You've been painting?'

Joel nodded. He took a gulp from the can and said, 'Just finished. Thought you were psychic.'

'I'm not psychic.'

'Celtic ancestry,' he said.

Amber, reflecting that she must be growing used to the odd way this man's mind worked, answered, 'Not that I know of.'

'Somewhere,' Joel insisted. 'How far back can you trace your family?'

'Not far. Red hair isn't exclusively Celtic, is it?'

'It isn't red.'

'Thank you,' Amber said with almost genuine gratitude. 'I wish you'd been around to tell my schoolmates that twenty years ago.'

'Twenty?'

'Something like that. I'm twenty-eight,' she added, answering his unspoken question.

Joel nodded. As he drank some more of the beer, Amber found herself watching the movements of his throat. She said, 'Have you been working non-stop?'

He gazed about vaguely as though searching for a calendar, then said, 'I guess.'

'You didn't answer your phone.'

He looked mildly astonished, as though she should have known he wasn't to be dragged from his work by anything as mundane as the telephone. 'I don't hear it in the studio,' he said.

Amber didn't say that he could have had an extension installed there. 'I have to return to Sydney next week,' she told him. 'I've been trying to contact you.'

She could have sworn that a shutter suddenly closed behind his eyes. 'Yeah, sorry,' he said. He lifted his hand again and drained the beer can. He wiped his mouth with his fingers, then sniffed at his stained shirt-sleeve. 'I stink,' he said, grimacing.

Amber didn't contradict him.

'I'll have a shower,' Joel decided, and stood up. 'Don't go,' he added, as Amber got out of her chair.

'Look, you're tired, if you'd just contact me when you're——'

'No,' he said. 'No, wait. I won't take long.'

'How much sleep have you had the last three days?' she demanded.

Joel grinned at her. 'Not much,' he confessed. 'It's OK. I won't sleep for hours anyway, I never do after finishing a painting. Have to unwind, I guess.' He touched her arm. 'Stay. Help yourself if you change your mind about the coffee. I've got one of those things that keeps it perking.'

When she heard the shower running in the bathroom, she got up and picked up the magazines he had dropped on the floor, making a space for them on top of the bookcase. She plumped cushions and tidied the top of the chest, and placed in the waste-paper basket she found behind the sofa a few screwed-up pieces of paper that had obviously been thrown not very accurately in its direction. Then she went into the kitchen.

A pile of coffee-cups was in the sink, but only one plate and a knife. Amber eyed them thoughtfully, found some detergent and a plug and began running hot water into the sink while she had a quick look in the small refrigerator. There was not much there—a few eggs, some stale bread, butter, a plastic pack of bacon, and some cheese, jam and honey.

While the dishes soaked she investigated the cupboards and refilled the coffee-machine. When Joel, apparently emerging from the bathroom, called, 'Amber?' she was drying the last of the cups, and answered,

'I'm making more coffee.'

'Yeah—fine,' he said, and unexpectedly appeared in the doorway of the kitchen, wearing nothing but a towel about his waist. He had shaved and his hair was slicked back. In spite of the broad bare chest sprinkled with dark hair, he looked unexpectedly boyish.

'You don't need to do that,' he protested, not very convincingly. 'You're cooking, too,' he added as the aroma of French toast, bacon and eggs reached him.

'You haven't eaten in days,' Amber accused. 'Have you?'

'Yes, I have,' he argued. 'I had bread and cheese and...' Like a little boy groping for excuses, he met her eyes with a guileless stare. 'Fruit!' he said triumphantly. 'Full of vitamins.'

'Get some clothes on,' Amber ordered him crisply, and turned her attention to the small stove.

She gave him time to find some in the chaos of his bedroom before she put the plate on the table, and he reappeared as if on cue, dressed in a clean pair of jeans and a creased, well-worn army-style shirt.

'What about you?' he asked, as she indicated he should sit down.

'I've just come from a very satisfying dinner,' she told him. 'Eat.'

'I will,' he said. 'It looks good. But I can't if you're going to stand over me.'

Amber went back into the kitchen and emerged with two cups of coffee. Placing one in front of Joel, she sat opposite him with the other, while he picked up the knife and fork she had set for him.

After the first mouthful he said, 'Tastes good. Who did you have dinner with? Harry?'

'How did you guess?'

He glanced up at her, his eyes unreadable. 'It wasn't hard.'

She sipped her coffee, telling herself there was no reason for her to explain to Joel Matheson what she did with her time or whom she spent it with. 'I wanted to talk to you about the exhibition,' she said.

'Did you have a good time?' He had finished the second mouthful and was sawing ferociously at a slice of bacon.

'What?'

'With Harry.' He looked up, his knife and fork poised. 'Did you have a good time?' Some flicker of expression crossed his face, lightened it. 'You ended the evening early.' His eyes were suddenly probing as they held her startled gaze.

'I had a lovely time, thank you,' Amber said, finding her voice. He was only making small talk, for heaven's sake. He didn't really *care* what she and Harry had done, or whether they had enjoyed it. 'I told you it was a very satisfying dinner. Delicious. And I did intend to have an early night, because I've had a tiring time of it, but when I saw your light on

I thought I'd try to talk to you because you've been hard to get hold of——'

'So you didn't go to Harry's place after dinner?'

'Yes, I did, as matter of fact, though what that has to do with——'

'You did?'

Amber didn't bother to answer the presumably rhetorical question. Nettled, she stared back at him as he regarded her with some attention.

'Harry must be slipping,' he said, and returned to his meal.

'Now, look!' Amber said firmly, holding on to her temper. 'What *you* may have in mind when you invite a woman to your apartment isn't necessarily true of every man. Harry and I are old friends——'

He cast her a derisive glance, swallowed the food he had been chewing and said, 'Yeah, so I saw the other day.'

'What you saw is none of your business! And neither is . . .'

'Whatever went on in Harry's apartment between the two of you.' Joel sighed. 'You're right. I was out of line.' He waved his knife despairingly.

'Yes, you were!' Amber agreed. 'Way out of line.' For some reason she was tempted to explain, but that would be like betraying Harry's confidence and, anyway, it *was* none of Joel's business.

'Let's not fight,' Joel begged. 'It'll give me indigestion.'

Amber closed her lips and waited until he had cleaned up the plate and started on his coffee.

'About the exhibition,' she said.

His nose buried in his coffee-cup, Joel grunted and lifted a shoulder. 'Yeah, well,' he said, replacing the cup on the table, 'I'm not so sure about that...'

'You agreed!' Amber reminded him, surprised at the depth of her angry anxiety.

'Did I?' His eyes met hers briefly, then slid away. 'I suppose I did,' he admitted.

'Then you can't go back on your word!'

'I'm not going back on it!' He seemed angry too, and Amber stopped herself, breathing calmly, keeping her temper under control.

She said, 'We need to make some arrangements, then.'

'Yeah. OK.' Joel dumped the coffee-cup on his plate, reached over for her empty cup too, and rose to take them to the kitchen. 'Thanks for the supper.'

'You're welcome.' Automatically Amber used the American phrase. She stood up, and, when he came back to the doorway of the kitchen, asked on impulse, 'May I see the new painting?' Perhaps that would get them back to an even keel, dispel the tension that seemed to be building between them without any reason.

She thought at first that Joel was going to refuse; then he said carelessly, 'I guess. Why not?' almost as though trying to convince himself there was no reason to turn down the request.

In the studio the painting was still on the easel. Joel flicked a switch, and a powerful bulb just above the easel lit the painting in a pitiless light. He said, 'It's not dry yet,' and stood just behind her as she looked at it from a few feet away.

'Oh!' Amber said softly, inwardly wincing. Remembering the dinner she had eaten so recently, the superbly cooked seafood mousse followed by delicately flavoured veal with asparagus and then a tray of perfectly ripened cheeses, all accompanied by the finest wines, she felt as though she had been punched in the stomach.

The pink savoury in all its ghastly glory had been preserved for posterity, lying on a white china plate, with a freshly gutted—or half-gutted—fish lying in a curve beside it, its glistening entrails sliding across the shining porcelain, its scales minutely detailed, silvery and so real that she could swear that if she touched it she would feel the sea-water still on them. But now the plate was not just lying as though on a table: it was being held by two desperately bony black hands, framed by emaciated arms, reminding Amber of every televised famine victim she had ever seen. The man's face was not in the picture, which included only the torso with every rib showing through the skin, but about the pathetically scrawny neck was a white collar and a black tie fashioned into a perfect, immaculate bow.

Amber studied it in silence, then turned to go to the window, looking blindly at the lights outside before facing the painting again, as though she had merely wanted to see it from further away. When she was sure her voice would be steady she said, 'I don't know if it will sell...unless to a public art gallery. Not many people want to own a painting that makes them feel guilty every time they look at it.'

Joel, staring sombrely at the canvas, said almost to himself, 'It isn't their guilt I'm painting. It's my own.'

He never talked about his painting, his motives, reasons, inspirations. For a moment Amber held her breath. Very quietly, so as not to disturb his mood, she said, 'Yours?'

'If I really cared,' he said, looking at her with angry eyes, 'if I really cared *enough*, I'd be out there doing something—in Ethiopia or somewhere—in Calcutta—hell, even on the streets of New York. There are enough people out there who need—God knows what they need. And there are so few who care enough to do something about it. And I sit in a studio,' he finished, 'and *paint* my conscience.'

'You have a talent,' she said. 'A talent that shouldn't be wasted. If you went to those places and painted them...perhaps you'd influence more people to help in some way...'

'Can you see it?' he asked her. 'Me setting up my easel and making pictures while people are *dying* all around me? Although that's what I'm doing, actually. Except that they're comfortably once removed—by the television or the newspaper. I can switch off or turn the page, and pretend they're not really there.'

'You're not alone,' she said. 'We're all of us doing the same thing. And as long as you paint pictures like this, we'll be reminded. That has to be a good thing. That makes people want to help—even if only by making a donation.'

'Yeah,' he said, digging his hands into his pockets, and scuffing at the floor. 'I suppose. Anyway——' He turned to her. 'If you sell this, the proceeds go to famine relief.'

Amber nodded. 'That's generous. It could fetch a lot.'

'It's not generous!' he almost snarled. 'It's a tiny smidgen of justice in an unjust world, that's all. It's a drop in the bucket.'

'It isn't *my* fault!' Amber reminded him. 'At least, not any more than anyone else's.'

'No, it isn't. The guilt is collective, so no one is responsible, and yet we all are.' He laughed suddenly, harshly. 'And you didn't come up here for a heavy philosophical discussion. I didn't intend to start one, either. Put it down to my mood.'

'You should be in a good mood. You've just finished a fine painting, even if the subject is . . . depressing.'

He gave her one of his sudden smiles. 'Don't mind me. I'm always like this when I've been working extra hard.'

'Moody?'

'I suppose you could call it that. It's either a tremendous high or the direct opposite. Sometimes both alternately. I'd be hell to live with. I *am* hell to live with. I've been told so on several occasions.'

Girlfriends, she supposed. With a sudden urge to change the subject, she said, 'Do you mind if I look at some of the pastels again?' At least they'd be more cheerful than . . . that. She glanced at the easel.

'Be my guest.' He opened the drawers for her himself.

After a while she sighed with a release of tension combined with sheer pleasurable excitement. 'They're even better than I remembered,' she said. 'I want more of these. Maybe a whole exhibition of them. In fact. . .' Her face aglow with the idea that had struck her, she turned to him. 'Why don't you come out to Australia and work there for a few months? If you can do these from memory, think what you might be able to achieve if you were actually on the spot!'

For a second she thought there was an answering glow in his eyes as he looked at her. Then it died, and he said flatly, 'No.'

His face closed up, and Amber felt as though she'd been slapped.

'No?' she said, her voice shrill with indignation. 'Just like that?'

'Just like that,' he echoed, and began putting the pastels back in the drawers.

'Think about it!' she urged him. 'These are so *good*! You must see that coming back home could be a catalyst—you could do *great* work there! I can help find you a studio, a place to live . . .'

'I'm not going, Amber.' He closed the last drawer and turned away.'

Amber caught at his sleeve. 'Why not?'

She hadn't thought he could look so cold. 'I don't need to give you a reason,' he said, pulling away from her.

'What happened to you?' she asked slowly, following him as he went towards the door to the narrow stair. 'Do you have bad memories of Australia?'

'In your own words,' he said, turning to give her a narrow grin that entirely lacked humour, 'it's none of your business.'

He opened the door and motioned for her to precede him down the steep stairway. Still seething with annoyed disappointment, she went too fast and in the dimness she slipped on the second-to-last stair and fell, twisting her ankle.

'*Ouch!*'

Joel was down beside her in a second, his hands on her shoulders. 'Are you all right?'

'Yes. I ricked my ankle, that's all,' she said, breathless with pain and feeling silly.

He helped her up. 'Sure it isn't sprained?'

'Yes, I'm sure.' She limped, but with his help managed to make it into the lounge, and let him put her on the sofa. 'I'll be fine in a minute,' she assured him.

Massaging the ankle, he looked at it frowningly and said, 'I think it's swelling a bit. I'll get some ice.'

He made quite an efficient compress with some ice cubes wrapped in a small towel and, crouching beside her, held it to her ankle.

'I'm sorry,' she said. 'That was stupid of me.'

Joel shook his head. 'Why are you so mad at me?'

'I'm not mad at you,' she said stiffly.

'You were. That's why you fell.'

'I am not mad at you,' Amber reiterated, emphasising every word.

Joel's gaze was disconcertingly direct, the more so because with her half lying on the sofa and him crouching at her side they were on a level and much too close for Amber's comfort. 'All right,' he said. 'Why is it so important that I should come to Australia with you?'

'Not *with* me, exactly,' she disclaimed.

'Don't split hairs. Just tell me why.'

'I told you, your...experimental work could—could develop there. I think you're ready to tackle a new direction, and the subjects that you've been using point to a readiness to return to your original environment. You've learnt a lot here, you've built up a reputation and you've developed a distinctive style.

But what are you, really? A minor New York artist——'

'Ow!'

'—when you have the potential to be a great Australian artist,' Amber finished.

Joel sat back on his heels. 'Are you saying I would be happier as a big fish in a little pond, instead of a little one in a big pond?'

'I'm saying you're an Australian, and maybe it's time you remembered that.'

'Patriotism?' Joel shook his head. With an air of self-mockery, he said, 'I prefer to be a citizen of the world.'

Amber said, 'You can't deny your roots, your background.'

'I'm not denying anything. It's a part of me, and it always will be. I just don't see that I have any particular obligation to make my work—indigenous.'

'Except the obligation that made you do those pastels,' Amber reminded him softly, but on a note of implacability. 'That came from inside you, didn't it?'

Joel made a quiet little scoffing sound. 'You,' he said, 'are reading a great deal into a few drawings.' He lifted the cloth and peered at her ankle. 'I don't think it's swelling any more. How does it feel?'

'I won't know until I stand on it.' Gingerly she swung her foot to the ground and Joel stepped back, watching her.

Amber walked a few steps. If she concentrated on ignoring the pain, she scarcely limped. 'I'm all right,' she said. 'Thank you for the first aid.'

'No problem.' He tossed the ice-filled cloth in his hand, then went into the kitchen and clattered the cubes into the sink.

'I'd better go,' she said when he came back. 'I wish you'd think about what I said, Joel.'

'It's four flights down. That ankle's still hurting, isn't it?'

'I'll manage.'

'You can stay if you like.' He waited until she looked at him, her gaze wary, and then added, grinning, 'I can sleep on the sofa.'

'That's very kind of you,' Amber told him serenely. 'But if you don't mind giving me your arm, I'm sure I can manage the stairs.'

CHAPTER FOUR

AMBER managed the first flight leaning on Joel's arm but at the landing he stopped and said, 'Maybe I should carry you.'

'No, thanks. I prefer hobbling to having you drop me down the stairs.'

Joel grinned. 'I was thinking of a fireman's lift.'

As he made to change his grip, she fended him off. 'Don't you dare!'

He laughed. 'It's still a long way down. Want to change your mind about staying?'

'No.' Her voice was firm. 'If we just take it slowly...'

He shrugged. 'Stubborn little cuss, aren't you?'

Amber didn't answer. She wasn't little and if she was on occasion stubborn it was a trait that had stood her in good stead. Stubbornness and flair were probably the qualities that got her furthest in business.

She had to stop again on the last landing, and Joel glanced at her and without warning swung her up in his arms. He silenced her protest by growling, 'Keep still and you'll be perfectly safe.'

It was a sensible if infuriating observation, and she lay stiff and still while he carried her the rest of the way to the street.

'Stay there,' he said, setting her on her feet in the doorway. 'I'll get you a cab.'

When he had, he said, 'Maybe I should come with you.'

'No!' Amber answered. 'You've been very kind,' she added, trying to sound gracious, 'but I'll be fine now, thank you. Really.'

He scowled, but let her go, slamming the door behind her and stepping back to lift a hand.

In the morning Amber woke late, and after glancing at her watch reached for the phone by the bed to order a room-service breakfast before heading for the shower.

Her hair felt sticky and lank and she washed it with the shampoo provided by the hotel, grabbing one towel to wrap about her head before she dried herself with the other and pulled on her silk wrap as she padded back into the bedroom.

She was vigorously rubbing the towel over her hair when she heard the soft tapping on the door.

Room service had been quick, she thought with surprise, going to open the door, then fell back with surprise as Joel walked into the room.

'What are you doing here at this hour?' she demanded crossly.

'How is it?' Joel asked.

'How is what?'

'Your ankle. I was worried about you.'

Conscious of her bare feet, the thin robe, the dishevelment of her hair and a total lack of make-up, she swallowed her enraged chagrin and said, 'Fine, thank you. I haven't even thought about it until now. You could have phoned.'

He hadn't taken his eyes off her face since closing the door. 'You might have lied. Your hair's a different colour.'

'I just washed it.'

'Yes, I can see.' He put out a hand to touch it and Amber flinched away.

'Sorry.' He dropped his hand. 'Walk.'

'What?'

'Walk. I want to be sure about your ankle.'

'I told you my ankle's fine. Nothing wrong with it.'

'Show me.'

Amber turned her back on him, and walked over to the table by the window, conscious of his eyes following her all the way. She swung round and walked back, stopping a few feet from him, not meeting his eyes.

'I wish you'd let me paint you,' he said.

'We've already discussed that.' She looked up.

'Sunlight,' he said. His eyes had an intent look that she recognised.

'Joel——'

He took the towel from her hand and, without looking, threw it on the bed.

'Joel——'

He held her arm in a firm grip and propelled her towards the window again.

'*Joel*!' Amber said. 'You are *not* going to paint me!'

For a moment she thought he hadn't heard her at all. He was looking at her, but she knew he was seeing a canvas, a palette of colours. Then his eyes changed, grew warmer and filled with laughter.

'Never?' he said coaxingly.

'Never.' It was meant to be firm, uncompromising. Why, then, did she sound breathless and unsure? Damn the man, he was trying to hypnotise her. She dragged her eyes away from his. 'Never,' she repeated, making her voice hard and steady. 'I am not going to let you bully me.'

'What if I beg?' he asked softly, his head on one side.

She could scarcely imagine it. Anyway, although he was doing his best to look pleading, laughter lurked in his eyes.

'No,' she said. 'No, and no, and no. Do I make myself clear?'

'OK.' He spread his hands and backed away from her. 'I get the message.'

Amber regarded him with suspicion. She had the feeling that he was giving in too easily.

A rap on the door made them both look towards it.

'My breakfast,' she said.

The waiter came into the room and placed the tray on the table by the window. He glanced at Joel and something flickered across his face. Amber handed the man a tip, then, as the door snapped shut behind him, swung round.

'You know what he thought,' she accused Joel.

He grinned. 'Does it matter? Come and have your breakfast.'

'Don't give me orders!'

'If you're afraid that Harry will find out——'

'I'm not afraid of anyone finding out. I just don't like——'

He was looking at her politely, waiting for her to finish what she was trying to say.

'Oh, never mind!' she sighed.

He shrugged, and took the covering napkin off the small basket on the tray. 'Smells good,' he said wistfully. 'Can you eat all that?'

Four slices of toast and two warm, fluffy croissants nestled in the basket. 'Have some,' she said resignedly. 'I'm going to dry my hair.'

She switched on the drier in the bathroom and in ten minutes was able to comb her hair into its usual sleek cap.

When she returned Joel was sitting comfortably on one of the chairs flanking the table, eyeing the coffeepot longingly as he finished off one of the croissants. Amber went back to the bathroom and picked up a glass tumbler from the shelf over the washbasin.

'Here,' she said, placing it in front of Joel. 'Help yourself.'

'Thanks.' He poured himself coffee and sipped it while she downed the small glass of orange juice and spread marmalade on the remaining croissant.

'Shall I pour some for you?' he asked her.

Amber nodded. He might as well make himself useful in some way.

She stirred sugar into the coffee and said, 'You'll have to go. I need to get dressed.'

'You look fine to me.' Joel ogled her outrageously.

'Stop that!'

He laughed. 'Just looking.'

'Well, you can stop!'

'It really bothers you, doesn't it?' he asked curiously, the laughter dying from his eyes.

'I don't find it funny.'

'I was teasing.' He put out a big hand, covering hers. 'Sorry.'

Amber smartly withdrew her hand. 'All right,' she said coldly.

Joel frowned. She removed her gaze from his searching scrutiny and said, pushing back her chair, 'I have an appointment.'

'OK. I'm going.' He got up slowly, still looking at her. 'How do you do that?'

'Do what?' Nonplussed, she looked at him again.

'Turn on the ice, just like that.' He snapped his fingers. 'And you with hair that colour, too.'

'The colour of my hair has nothing to do with my temperament,' she informed him. 'That's nothing but an old wives' tale.'

But his gaze had shifted, and, as though he hadn't heard her, he added softly, 'And that mouth.'

He raised a finger and touched her lips briefly, unexpectedly.

Amber whipped her head away and stepped back.

Joel held her eyes, a sudden, interested light in his. He came closer, coming after her.

'Amber?' he said, his voice scarcely more than a murmur.

'You said you were going.'

'Do you want me to?'

Amber realised that if she kept backing from him she would come up against the bed. She stood her ground. 'Yes. I told you, I have to see someone.'

'Harry?' he asked.

'No, not Harry.'

He was standing just in front of her. She wanted to push him away. She didn't want to touch him.

He lifted a hand, curling it about her nape.

Amber's eyes flashed. She raised her hand and chopped his arm away from her.

For a moment a spark of anger lit his eyes, too, but it quickly died. He turned abruptly and went to the door. 'See you,' he said casually, and let himself out.

Amber's time in New York was running out. She had acquired a few paintings for her gallery, and arranged for them to be sent to her in Sydney, and had sold some prints she had brought with her. But the arrangements still needed to be made for Joel's exhibition, and she was determined to persuade him to come too.

'I don't know why he doesn't want to,' Harry said, when she asked him. 'Although he's never been back there since he came to America, has he?'

'Apparently not. Do you think you might be able to persuade him? I'm sure it would be good for his painting.'

'Why?'

'I just feel it. He's ready for it.'

'Female intuition?' Harry teased.

'Not female intuition so much as experience with artists. When they take a new direction as he has, I think it should be encouraged.'

'Are you sure it is a genuine new direction? Scenes from his childhood? It could be just a nostalgia trip. Taking a breather between more demanding projects.'

'I don't think so. There's something else there—something that needs to be explored, worked through...'

'You want me to talk to him?'

'If you think you can persuade him.'

Harry shrugged. 'I can try. Though why I should, when you're planning to take away one of my best artists...'

Amber smiled at him. 'I don't intend to take him away forever. And if he did decide to stay, he could still send you some of his paintings. He'd probably get better prices here.'

'Well, I'm expecting him to come in some time to see how the exhibition is going. I'll mention it.'

But Harry had no luck either. 'He says he doesn't want to go and that's it,' he reported. 'No reasons, just a blank refusal to think about it.'

Amber sighed. 'Well, thanks for trying. At least he's agreed to let me show his work. I'll have to see him about that. Maybe I can talk him round.'

She phoned Joel, and this time he answered almost immediately, and made a time for her to come and see him at the studio.

When he opened the door he stood for a moment simply looking at her, almost as though he had forgotten who she was. He was wearing a shirt that was tucked into his jeans but not buttoned, and his feet were bare.

'We had an appointment,' she reminded him.

'Yeah, I know.' He passed a hand over his hair, scowling. 'OK.' He stood aside with some reluctance, and let her in.

Amber paused a few steps into the living-room, realising that there was another occupant. A girl lounged on the sofa, pink-tipped toes propped on one of its black leather arms, a mane of glorious blonde hair spilling over a cushion at the other end. A scarlet shirt was jauntily tied under her small, pointed breasts, and a short skirt showed off her long, tanned legs. A pair of scarlet high-heeled sandals lay on the floor beside her. The blue gaze she turned on Amber was definitely annoyed.

'This is Trudi,' Joel said. 'Trudi, this is Amber. She's an art dealer from Australia.'

Trudi, without moving an inch, inspected the new-comer, then, apparently deciding that this was no competition, gave her a dazzling smile. 'Hi!'

'Hello,' Amber said.

'Trudi's a neighbour,' Joel said.

'I model for Joel sometimes,' Trudi offered.

Amber smiled. 'Oh, yes?' she said politely.

Joel said, transferring his gaze to the girl, 'Amber and I have business to discuss. I don't want to be rude, but...'

'OK.' Trudi sighed, pouted, and sat up, wriggling her bottom round on the sofa so that her skirt rode even further up on her thighs while she fished with her painted toenails for her shoes. 'I can take a hint.'

'Sit down, Amber,' Joel invited.

She sat, finding a miraculously empty chair. Joel opened the door for Trudi, exchanging a murmured word or two as the girl briefly rested a hand on his chest, then closed the door and turned to Amber. 'Sorry about that.'

'It's all right,' Amber said stiffly. She wondered what the girl's parents thought of her modelling for Joel. She looked about half his age. On impulse she added, 'I didn't know you were... working.'

He was standing with his feet apart, his thumbs hooked in his belt, looking at her. He smiled. 'If I'd been working, I'd have been up in the studio.'

'I see.'

'Do you?' he drawled. There was laughter in his eyes.

Amber looked away, picking up the briefcase she had brought with her. 'Perhaps we could go up to the studio,' she suggested freezingly. 'I'd like to make a complete list of what I want for the exhibition.'

When they had finished, he offered a cup of coffee, and Amber accepted because the most difficult part was yet to come. When he had seated himself on the sofa, facing her, with a steaming cup in his hand, she took a deep breath, and said, 'I still want you to come to Sydney. The art without the artist is...incomplete.'

His face closed, and she said, 'Listen to me, please,' and launched into her well prepared argument.

He heard her out, his eyes on her face as he sipped at his coffee. And when she had finished he put down his cup and said, 'I already told you, I'm not coming.'

'Why not?'

'I don't have to give you reasons.'

'I'd like to hear some, all the same.'

Joel stood up. 'Look, if you don't want to take the pictures after all...'

Shooting to her feet, Amber said, 'I want the pictures, and I want you!'

The look he slanted at her would have been enough to make her blush if she'd been Trudi's age. 'Now that's an interesting statement!'

'You know what I mean!' she told him. 'And stop looking at me like that! I'm not one of your nymphet models!'

Joel's eyebrows rose. 'And what do mean by that, exactly?'

The inexplicable anger she had been tamping down ever since she arrived rose to the surface, irresistibly. 'You know perfectly well!' she snapped. 'You ought to be ashamed of yourself! How old is Trudi, anyway?'

'Is that any of your business?' he asked. His voice was so mild that it was almost absent-minded, but there was a gleam in his eyes that should have warned her.

'Is she the real reason you don't want to leave New York?' she asked scathingly.

'No,' Joel replied coolly. 'You are.'

She was surprised at how much it hurt, even though she had to admit she couldn't blame him. She had never been as nice to him as she'd kept telling herself she ought to be. And he must have got tired of hoping she'd change. She said, hardily, 'You shouldn't let your likes and dislikes get in the way of business.'

'Is that your philosophy?' he asked.

Amber shrugged. 'More or less. You needn't see much of me, once you're there. I'm sure we can work it out.'

'No.'

'Oh, for crying out loud!' Amber exclaimed. 'What do I have to do to convince you?'

He grinned. 'Is that an offer?' He took a step towards her.

'No, it isn't! And you can keep your cheap shots—and your hands—to yourself!'

Instead, he reached out long arms and grabbed her, bringing her close to him. The grin was still on his face. 'I might be open to that sort of offer,' he said.

'Stop it, Joel!' She knew he wasn't serious. He was just trying to keep her off balance. She pushed against his chest. 'Let me go.'

'I don't think I want to.'

'Too bad. Let me go.' She looked into his eyes, keeping her gaze, she hoped, cool and implacable.

He searched her face. 'Is that what you really want?'

Her pulses were doing crazy things. Her voice was annoyingly husky. 'Yes.' She curled her hands into fists and pushed again. It made no difference. He was as immovable as rock. 'Joel . . .'

'Don't you ever think about anything but business?' he asked.

'Not with artists.'

'With Harry?'

'I'm not going to explain our relationship to you. That's between Harry and me.'

'And this?' he asked. His voice had gone husky, too. His eyes held hers. 'Between you and me?'

She swallowed. 'There's nothing—you just said you don't like me.'

He scowled at her. 'I never said anything of the kind!'

'As good as. You don't want to come to Australia because of me——'

He let her go then, with startling suddenness. 'For an intelligent woman,' he fumed, still scowling, 'you say some bloody silly things.'

'You were the one who said it! Half the time you don't make any sense, anyway,' she informed him. 'You seem to be constitutionally incapable of talking like a rational human being.'

'And you seem incapable of thinking like one!'

'Me?' The injustice of it! 'If I weren't a particularly rational person,' she said indignantly, 'I'd have thrown something at your head by now!'

The scowl lifted from his face, and he broke into laughter. 'Try it some time,' he said, looking down at her, 'and see what you get.'

Games, she thought, staring defiantly into his eyes. He was obviously an expert, in spite of his earlier denial. She took a deep breath, contemplating her next move.

But he got in first. Taking her totally by surprise, he said, 'Tell you what. I'll come on one condition.'

As she opened her mouth, her eyes wary, he held up his hand. 'No, not that,' he said reprovingly. 'Seriously—I'll come to your exhibition if you'll let me do a picture of you.'

CHAPTER FIVE

'THE man's crazy,' Amber told her assistant a few days later.

Dinah Mangan brushed dark hair back from her brown eyes and looked up at her employer curiously as she stripped the wrapping from a painting which had just arrived at the Sydney gallery. Dinah always asked about the artists Amber met on her buying trips, and Amber was happy to oblige with pithy descriptions. 'Crazy? In what particular way?'

Amber searched for words. 'He's—rude, for one thing,' she said. 'And self-centred,' she added, suppressing a twinge of conscience. He had, after all, been quite concerned about her ankle.

Briskly she twisted a piece of string around her fingers and tucked in the end.

Dinah grimaced. 'One of those. Thinks because he's talented he can treat other people like dirt?'

'No,' Amber admitted, being fair. 'It's not like that. He just gets so absorbed up in his work, I think he has trouble finding room in his head for other things. He wants to paint me,' she said, and then turned away quickly. She hadn't meant to tell anyone that.

Dinah said, 'I didn't know he did portraits.'

'I don't know if it's a portrait he has in mind,' Amber admitted uneasily. She didn't even know why she had in the end succumbed to what she had told him roundly amounted to blackmail. Only he was adamant that it was the only condition on which he was willing to come to Sydney.

Dinah was saying, 'At least Matheson isn't likely to paint you with two eyes on one side of your head, and a breast tucked under your armpit.'

'He'll probably never paint me at all,' Amber said hopefully. 'By the time he gets here he'll be off on some new tack.'

She laughed suddenly, and when Dinah asked curiously, 'What?' she told her the story of the pink pastry and how she'd been left holding it because Joel had taken a fancy to paint the thing.

She wrote him very businesslike letters about the proposed showing, and received back disjointed, scrawled notes. Once when she hadn't had a reply to a query about dates, and couldn't rouse Joel on the telephone, she faxed an appeal to Harry, asking him to do her a favour and try to get Matheson to contact her.

She was working late when the call came through. She had been just about to pack up and go home, and before she touched the receiver she knew it would be Joel. She took a couple of steadying breaths before she lifted it.

'Amber!' he said in answer to her crisp,

'Glenora Gallery.'

'Yes,' she said, although she was well aware he had not doubted her identity. There was no mistaking his voice, either.

'What are you doing?' he demanded.

'I'm about to go home,' she told him. 'What have *you* been doing for the past two weeks? I've been trying to get hold of you——'

'I know. You want pictures, don't you?'

She sighed. 'Yes, I want pictures.'

'Well, then. What time is it there?'

She told him, after glancing at her watch.

He said, 'And you're just closing up?'

'No, we've been closed for hours. But there's a lot to do, I've two more exhibitions scheduled as well as yours, and artists who don't reply to their mail or answer phone calls make extra work——'

'OK. I guess I should have got back to you,' he mumbled.

'Are the dates all right?' she asked, slightly mollified. 'Because if not I can juggle one of the others——'

'The dates'll be fine,' he said. Why did she get the feeling he couldn't even remember what they were at this point? 'You sound tired,' he added. 'Why don't you get some sleep?'

'That's exactly what I intended.'

He laughed. 'How do you get home?'

'I have a car. It's parked just outside.'

'Take care. I want you in one piece when I paint you. And don't cut your hair.'

And, before she could answer that, he had hung up.

The pastels arrived before him. Knowing his preference for hanging his work himself, she left them in the crates, and on the day he was due sent Dinah to the airport to meet him.

'Don't you want to go?' Dinah asked her.

'I've too much to do,' Amber told her. 'Get him paged. Not that he's hard to find. He's big enough. And he'll either be standing around like a lost sheep or surrounded by admiring females.'

Dinah cast her a slightly surprised look. She seldom heard that waspish note in her employer's voice. 'Do I bring him here or take him straight to his hotel?' she asked.

'The hotel,' Amber answered hastily. 'He'll be exhausted, for one thing. Tell him to get rested, and to give us a call here tomorrow when he feels up to helping to uncrate his stuff and hang it.'

But when Dinah arrived back Joel was trailing behind her like a dog that had slipped its leash. And looking just as pleased with himself.

'Dinah, I told you——' Amber began, rising from her desk to confront him.

Dinah said breathlessly, 'He said he wanted——'

And Joel cut in, 'I wanted to see you first.'

'Why, is there a problem?' Amber was at her most cool. 'I'm sure Dinah can——'

'Dinah's been great,' Joel said, and turned his smile on for the girl's benefit. 'Thank you, Dinah.'

She beamed back at him, as he gently steered her out the door and shut it behind her. Amber looked on resignedly. Another easy conquest. Dinah was a pretty young woman and she had a very nice steady boyfriend. She was far too sensible to let Joel go to her head, but she obviously wasn't immune to the switched-on charm.

It seemed to have been switched off again now. He leaned against the door and regarded Amber critically. 'I told you not to cut your hair,' he said.

'I haven't,' she answered through gritted teeth, 'since you *instructed* me not to.' She'd been tempted to go straight out and get a crew-cut, but wisdom had prevailed. She didn't want him reneging on the exhibition.

'Mm,' he said in a dissatisfied tone. 'I'd like it longer.' His gaze roved over her dress, and then back to her eyes. Meeting their green glare, he grinned. She could almost see him deciding not to say anything about her businesslike navy-and-white. 'How are you, anyway?' he asked, his tone almost coaxing as he moved away from the door.

'Fine, thank you.' She held her ground even when he came round the desk and stood close enough to touch her. 'And you?' she asked politely.

'Fine.' His tone was absent. He bent suddenly and gave her a quick, warm kiss on her surprised mouth. 'Fine,' he repeated, as she recoiled as far as she could, jammed between chair and desk. 'That was for Harry,' he said blandly. 'He asked me to give you his love.'

'Thank you,' she said.

'And this,' he added, 'is for me.' And he took her face between his big hands and kissed her again—quite thoroughly, but not for long, because she pushed him away with her fists against his chest, making a furious sound in her throat.

He stepped back, cocking his head to one side, his brows rising. 'No?'

'No!' Amber held the back of her chair to steady herself. 'You're taking too much for granted.'

He shrugged. 'Sorry.' His eyes were assessing, puzzled and perhaps slightly disbelieving.

'And you need a shave,' she reminded him meanly.

Fingering the slight, stubbly shadow on his chin, he asked, 'Did I scratch you?' He inspected the creamy skin of her face. 'We could try again tomorrow,' he suggested.

'We won't do anything of the kind!' Amber snapped. 'Tomorrow we're hanging your pastels, anyway. And even if we weren't——'

'There's always the evening,' he said. 'We'll deserve a good dinner after that.'

'Ask Dinah,' she advised him, and then wondered what Dinah's boyfriend would have to say about that.

'I'm asking *you*,' Joel said. 'And Dinah, if you like. I guess she'll appreciate a decent meal, too, after a hard day's work.'

In the end it was a foursome. Dinah's boyfriend came to fetch her, and stayed to help with the hanging, and when Amber decided to call it a day they freshened up and went out to an all-night café. It was after midnight when they left the place, and Amber said, 'I'll drop you off at your hotel, Joel.'

'Thanks a lot, Joel,' Dinah said as her boyfriend dropped an arm about her shoulders and added his thanks too. They had obviously had a great time in spite of being tired, and Amber had seen a new side to Joel. It had been a fairly hilarious evening at times, but she'd also glimpsed a quite startling intelligence behind the lazy charm.

'It was good of you to pay for us all,' Amber told him as he folded his legs into the car beside her. 'Thank you.'

'It's good of you to take me home,' he answered. 'I knew you were a nice girl underneath.'

She didn't answer that, concentrating on getting the car started and into the stream of night-time traffic.

After a while he said quietly, 'Have I offended you again?' and his hand brushed aside the fall of hair that touched her jawline and hid her face from him.

She shied away, shaking her head to disguise the instinctive reaction. 'Of course not. I'm getting used to your...mannerisms.'

'What a word. You think I'm precious?'

'You're not precious at all. I suppose you're just...honest. Aren't you?'

He said, 'I guess. I don't really think about it.'

'All you really think about is your art, isn't it?'

'I've thought about *you* a lot, lately.'

She wasn't looking at him. Her hands on the wheel tightened. 'You still want to paint me?'

'That's why I'm here.'

'Not the only reason!' She'd wondered if he'd really been serious about that strange bargain.

'Painting you?' he said. 'No, not the only reason. You know that.'

'I don't know——' She broke off and braked sharply as a car careened out of a nearby street and did a fast U-turn in front of them. '*Idiot!*'

Joel was sitting up straight. She changed gear and proceeded cautiously after the receding tail-lights. 'I have to concentrate,' she said, and he lapsed into total silence.

When she drew up outside the hotel, he said, 'Come in for a nightcap?'

'No, thanks. I'd have to find a place to park first, and anyway I've got to work tomorrow.'

'I'll come over and help you finish,' he said. 'Don't bother picking me up. I'll walk.'

She kept her hands clamped on the wheel, and he hesitated, then touched her cheek with his fingers and climbed out, closing the door firmly behind him.

* * *

When all the pictures were finally hung, she let Dinah
go early, and she and Joel stowed the last of the pack-
aging in the big storage-room in the basement.

While he was washing his hands, she took a bottle
of sherry from a cupboard in her office and poured
some into two glasses. 'I thought we'd drink to the
success of the exhibition,' she said when he joined
her. 'Shall we wander round and make sure everything's hung the right way up?'

They did so with their glasses in their hands. It
wasn't a large exhibition; the gallery was modest, but
made interesting by being on three levels, the third
one reached by a winding wrought-iron stair. Grey
walls backgrounded the ochres and oranges and dusty
sunlight colours of the pastels, and in some places she
had draped yards of coarse sacking behind the pictures. It seemed to her to go with the peeling bark of
the gum trees, the rusted tins in the foreground of the
one of the pictures, and the sturdy country people
with battered wide-brimmed hats and rolled shirt-
sleeves or faded printed dresses who featured in a good
many of them.

On the lower levels there were a couple of grey
leather loungers for viewers to sit on, but on the upper
level only huge coloured scatter cushions. It was
hardly possible to get large items of furniture up the
stairs. When they reached that level, with Amber in
the lead and Joel following, he slumped down on the
cushions and looked up at her, his half-emptied glass
in his hand. 'Join me?' he invited, patting a cushion
beside him.

Amber shook her head, and went over to one of
the pictures, shifting a corner up and then down again.

She stepped back, staring at it, and Joel said, 'It's straight. So are all of them. Why are you so nervous around me?'

She glanced at him and edged further away, gazing at a family group with a couple of horses, standing by a water-hole. The largest part of the canvas, at the top, was taken up by the vast expanse of country beyond the group, and the way the father was staring into the distance seemed to indicate that they had a long way to go. She said, 'Where are they going?'

'Wherever,' he replied. He sounded bored.

Amber turned. 'Don't you know?'

'Don't you?' he countered. He was lying on his stomach now among the cushions, surveying the remainder of his sherry with a disgruntled expression.

She looked at the picture again. There was a gaunt toughness about the man, a grim determination. Beside him, his wife's shoulders drooped as she bent over a baby in her arms, half turned away from her husband. Another child clung at her skirts, looking up. 'Into an uncertain future, I'd say,' Amber guessed.

Joel said, 'Aren't we all? When can I paint you?'

'You don't really want——'

He sat up. 'I do really want! Don't you welsh on me now!'

'I just didn't think that——'

'No, you don't much, do you?'

Amber contemplated the sherry still in her glass, and decided regretfully that it wasn't enough to do any damage if she threw it at him. She said, 'You are the most bad-mannered man I've ever——'

'Honest,' Joel argued. 'You said I was honest, before.'

'And bad-mannered. The two are not mutually exclusive.'

He put down his glass carefully on the floor and looked at her equally carefully. 'You're angry again.'

'How did you guess?'

Joel grinned. 'You get green glass chips in your eyes.'

'That's a ridiculous thing to say!'

'I don't see why. It's true.'

'It isn't true, it's a mere——'

'How do you know?' he reasoned. 'You can't see them.'

'—metaphor!'

'My, what big words you know, Red Riding Hood!'

'And you've got that wrong, too!' Amber said triumphantly.

'Well, I don't see you as Grandmother,' he explained. 'What with that red cap and all. But I have a feeling you've cast me as the wolf.'

Amber gave a ladylike snort and finished her sherry. 'Don't be silly!'

'Well, why don't *you* stop being silly and come and sit down for a while?' he suggested. 'You must be tired. I know I am.'

'You probably still have jet lag.' She walked warily towards the cushions and he sat up and held out his hand, drawing her down into the curve of his arm.

Amber sat stiffly, her eyes on the wall in front of them and the pictures that hung on it. 'I think they'll sell,' she said. 'They won't make people uncomfortable——'

'They should.'

'—at first,' she finished.

He looked down at her. 'You noticed,' he said softly.

'If I hadn't, I wouldn't have wanted to show them,' she said. 'I'm not interested in sentiment.'

He asked mildly, 'What's wrong with sentiment?'

She shrugged, but the hand on her shoulder didn't budge. 'You know what I mean,' she said. 'Pap for the masses.'

'I'm all for a bit of pap now and then, myself. Ice-cream or gooey chocolate makes a nice change to a diet of good red meat and raw vegetables.'

'You don't paint pap.'

He moved restlessly by her side. 'Sometimes I wish I could.'

'I think I can understand that.'

'Can you?' He was looking down at her, and his eyes were dark and brooding. His free hand came up and he gentled the hair from her cheek, as he had in the car the night before. The arm about her shoulder tightened. His fingers turned her face up to him, and after the barest hesitation he kissed her.

It was a soft but not tentative kiss. He seemed to want to find out the exact shape of her mouth, before proceeding any further. And when he did she felt her lips parting and her head tipping back against his arm. She had her eyes closed, but the room seemed to spin silently about them, so that she almost lost her balance.

And then he lowered her to the cushions, still kissing her with that insistent, seductive tenderness, and one hand was behind her, the other sliding down her tautened throat to rest just inside her blouse, the fingers curved over the warm skin of her shoulder, the thumb caressing a heavily beating pulse.

He lifted his head, and she opened her eyes, saw his blazing under half-closed lids, and then his hand shifted to the top button of her blouse, flicking it out of the buttonhole, and his mouth went to her throat while his fingers fiddled with another button.

Amber gasped, 'Joel, no! Stop!'

For a moment she thought he was going to ignore her. His mouth was open on her skin, and his hand was skimming the swell of her breast. She put her hands on his shoulders, shoving at him, and his hand went back to her throat, his head jerking up, his eyes wide now, very bright, and questioning.

'Amber?' he said.

'Let me up.' She was still pushing against him. 'Let me go, Joel.'

He looked puzzled. 'Are you sure?'

'Yes, I'm sure!' she said crossly. 'You great oaf, get off me!'

He got up then, and watched as she scrambled to her feet after him, and smoothed her hair. Not looking at him, she bent to pick up the two wine glasses, wondering if she could blame the sherry for her unexpected behaviour.

As if reading her mind, Joel said, 'You're not going to tell me it was the drink doing the kissing.'

'*You* were doing the kissing!' she retorted, as she made for the stairs.

'I did have help,' he argued. 'Be careful on those stairs.'

She had started down the stairs at a reckless pace, but she was used to them and reached the bottom without mishap. 'Don't read too much into it.'

'Tell me,' he invited as they reached the little kitchenette and she put the glasses by the sink, 'what I should read into it.'

She turned, to find him looming over her, his hands on either side trapping her against the counter. 'A mild celebration,' she said, fighting down panic, 'in honour of your exhibition.'

'Do you celebrate with all your artists that way?'

'Of course not!' For the life of her she couldn't think of anything more to say.

He smiled then. 'Good,' he said, and took his hands away, moving back from her. 'I didn't think so.'

CHAPTER SIX

THE opening was more successful than even Amber had dared hope for. Joel, astonishingly, had his hair trimmed for the occasion, and turned up wearing a striped shirt and fitting trousers. He looked magnificent, and Amber wasn't the only woman who thought so. They gathered round him like flies.

She herself was kept busy greeting people and making sure that those who could afford to buy were encouraged to do so. In the first hour she and Dinah had already placed red stickers on several pictures.

She had just emptied a glass of champagne when Joel's hand closed on her arm, and he said, 'Here's someone who's been looking for you, Amber.'

She turned and saw first Joel's eyes, more alert than usual as he watched her, and then Harry's easy smile.

'Hello, Amber.' Harry bent to kiss her cheek.

'Harry! What are you doing here?'

Harry turned to Joel. 'You didn't tell her I was coming?'

'Thought it would be a nice surprise,' Joel said blandly. 'It is, isn't it, Amber?'

'Yes, of course.' She smiled at Harry. 'How long can you stay?'

'I'm giving myself a holiday. Couple of weeks. Never visited this country before. Maybe I'll find another Joel Matheson while I'm here.'

'I thought you said a holiday,' she teased.

Joel put a hand on Harry's shoulder. 'We'll have to show you round, won't we, Amber?'

Amber glanced at him with faint suspicion. What was he up to?

She didn't have time to work it out. Someone hovered at her side, and she had to turn away to discuss another sale.

Harry was still there when everyone except Joel and Amber had gone. 'Where are you staying?' she asked him.

'The same hotel as Joel. I got him to book a room for me.'

'Why don't we all go out to supper?' Joel suggested. 'Or back to our hotel for a nightcap?'

'Harry must be tired,' Amber objected. 'And so am I, actually. I'll drop you both off.'

Driving away from the hotel afterwards, she wondered again what Joel was up to. A nice surprise, he had said. Well, maybe. She just had a very strong feeling that he'd had some ulterior motive. Only for the life of her she couldn't work out what it might be.

The feeling became even stronger over the next two weeks. Amber was very busy with the exhibition. Joel constituted himself Harry's unofficial tour guide, and whisked him off on a day trip to the Blue Mountains, then to a weekend on the Gold Coast, and even accompanied him on a tourist flight to Alice Springs and Ayers Rock.

No sooner had they returned from there than Joel booked three seats for the latest production at the Opera House and played host to both Harry and Amber for the evening. Wearing evening clothes, he was stunning, although he spoiled the effect somewhat after the interval by pulling off his bow-tie and stuffing it into his pocket.

At supper afterwards, he seemed to notice Amber's green silk dress for the first time, and gave a grunt of what appeared to be appreciation. 'That's an improvement,' he said, eyeing her bared shoulders. 'Your hair looks better, too.'

It had got to the in-between stage, too short to put up but long enough to be in the way when she bent her head over an account or wore a dress with a collar. 'It's a nuisance,' she said. 'How long do you want it?'

'Longer than that. I want it round your shoulders.'

Harry was looking slightly mystified, and Amber explained, 'Joel thinks he wants to paint me.'

'Really?'

He didn't need to look quite so surprised, she felt, as Joel said aggressively, 'I don't *think* I want to paint you. I'm going to paint you. You've agreed.'

'Yes, all right,' she admitted shortly.

'When was that, Amber?' Harry asked.

'When I said I'd come to Sydney for the opening,' Joel told him. 'She reckons it's blackmail.' He gave her a lazy smile.

'Oh, I don't think you can call it that,' Harry murmured, looking with some curiosity from him to Amber and back again. 'Undue pressure, maybe. I'd like to see it when it's done.'

Joel looked at him and shrugged.

And Amber said, 'Why don't you let me off the hook, Joel? You're not a portrait painter, and you've had your fun.'

Harry's brows silently rose, and Joel said, 'You're giving Harry the wrong idea, Amber. What "fun" are you talking about?'

Impatiently, she said, 'You know perfectly well you only said that to put me off. You thought I wouldn't agree, and you could get out of coming over here. Well, I called your bluff, but you needn't waste time doing a picture of me. Portraits aren't your style, and we all know it.'

Joel leaned over the table towards her, his eyes bright with temper, although his deep voice was quite soft. 'You're not getting away with that. You said you'd let me paint you, and I'm damn well going to. And, for your information, I can do just as good a portrait of you as any other artist you can name, if I so choose! Better!'

Amber took a breath. 'All right, I didn't mean to impugn your ability. If you're going to insist on going through with this farce——'

'Farce?' Joel's palm descended on the table, rattling their plates.

Harry put a hand on his arm, his bright, interested eyes sliding to Amber's flushed face. 'Steady on, Joel,' he said mildly. 'Amber just said she's not doubting your talent.'

'Only his sanity,' Amber snapped. 'Honestly, once he's got an idea in his head, he's like a dog with a long-lost bone. What's the *point* in painting me?'

'What's the point in painting anything?' Joel growled. 'And *you* make your living from selling art works!' he added witheringly.

'I'd say you're a very paintable woman,' Harry observed, rather heavy-handedly, she thought. 'If I had the talent, I'd like to paint you myself.'

Amber swallowed her instinctive desire to snarl, and smiled at him instead. 'Thank you, Harry, dear.' She injected as much sincerity as she could into her voice.

'Huh!' Joel exclaimed.

Harry looked slightly pained, and Amber demanded sweetly, 'What's that, Joel?'

He was shaking his head almost sorrowfully at Harry. 'You don't know her the way I do. You'd paint her looking pink and pretty.'

'You scarcely know me at all!'

But even Harry wasn't listening. 'No.' He looked at Amber consideringly. 'Green, maybe. Like that dress. A sort of woodland nymph?'

Joel snorted. 'Nymph!' he repeated scornfully.

Tempted to try a snort of her own, Amber said, 'If you two have quite finished——'

'You don't fancy yourself as a nymph?' Joel enquired maliciously.

Harry said, 'Sorry, Amber. I didn't mean anything insulting——'

'I know.' She gave him a warm smile. 'I'm flattered, of course,' she managed, aware of Joel's open disbelief. 'I have to admit I...h-hadn't thought of myself in that light,' she added, kicking Joel accurately under the table as she saw his shoulders begin to shake.

He drew in his breath and sent her an indignant look which she managed to ignore.

'So how are you going to paint her?' Harry asked.

'I haven't decided.' Joel's face was quite deadpan now. 'Maybe as a tiger-cat.'

'A clichéd idea, surely,' Amber said coldly.

'The golden African variety,' Joel was saying, as though he hadn't heard her. 'Small and fierce.'

Amber did snort then, in a genteel way. '*Very* clichéd.'

'I've never thought of you as fierce, Amber,' Harry said, obviously intrigued.

'Joel is letting his artist's imagination run away with him,' she said.

Ignoring her again, Joel asked, 'What *did* you think?'

'A very together lady,' Harry replied. 'Cool, clever, sharp as a tack. But fierce?' He studied Amber, his head cocked. 'No. Not the right word, Joel.'

Joel's lip curled. 'A lot you know——'

Amber forcefully interrupted. 'If you two male chauvinists don't mind, I think I'd like to go now.'

Harry looked guilty and immediately apologised. Joel just grinned and rose indolently from the table, padding after them as Harry opened the street door for Amber.

'Isn't that male chauvinist behaviour?' he enquired.

'It's polite behaviour,' Amber told him. 'Something you know nothing about.'

He laughed.

Harry came to the gallery the next day to bear her off for lunch. 'It'll be a late one,' she warned him. 'I can't leave Dinah alone when the gallery's busy. Joel's pastels are bringing crowds.'

When she joined him at last, she said, 'Where is Joel, by the way?'

'My Siamese twin? I told him I wanted to buy souvenirs for my children. Even Joel soon got sick of following me about while I pretended to shop. He caught sight of a real-estate agent's window and said he was going to look for a studio to rent.'

'He has been keen to give you a good time,' Amber said.

'Hmm. Last night I began to think he had another motive in mind.'

Before she could take him up on that, he asked her where she would like to eat and she suggested a small Greek restaurant where she sometimes took business contacts for a meal. 'It's just a short walk, and they serve great salads.'

Once there, Harry took charge and secured them a table almost hidden in a corner behind a huge potted palm. They were on to strong aromatic coffee before he mentioned Joel again. 'What's going on between you two?' he asked her bluntly.

Just as bluntly, Amber answered, 'Nothing.'

Harry directed a shrewd look at her. 'That's not the impression I got last night. And why do *you* think Joel's so eager to keep me busy every minute of the day—and night?'

'He wants you to enjoy our holiday, I suppose,' Amber mumbled. 'And nothing happened last night that could possibly give you the impression that Joel and I are—that we have some kind of relationship.'

'Except the sparks flying across that table.'

'Nonsense. If there were any sparks flying, it was because we don't like each other.'

'Oh, no? I'm sure that's not true of Joel, anyway. I'd say he liked you quite a lot from the first time he saw you. Although I admit he has odd ways of showing it.'

Amber pushed away her cup. 'He made a pass in New York, I turned him down, and he decided he didn't like me after all.'

'Is that true?'

'Yes.' It wasn't the whole truth, but the edited version was true enough. 'When I asked him to come here for the opening, he said he didn't want to, because of me. I'd wounded his ego, I suppose.'

Harry blinked. 'Doesn't sound like Joel to me. Are you sure that's what he meant?'

'Is there anything else he could have meant?' Amber demanded.

Doubtfully, Harry said, 'I don't know. But then why does he want to paint you?'

'Because he's pigheaded enough to cut off his nose to spite his face any day of the week.'

Harry shook his head. 'I think you've got it wrong. But I didn't ask you to have lunch with me so we could talk about Joel. I did want to know how things stood with you two, because . . . well, have you considered at all about what I said to you before you left New York?'

He had taken her hand in his, and alarm bells were ringing in her mind. 'Yes, of course,' she said hastily, her conscience reminding her that she had hardly given it a single thought. 'Do you mean you were really serious?'

'Never more so. We could have a good life together, Amber. At least, I think so. I'm talking about marriage, you know,' he reminded her, 'not a temporary arrangement of any sort.'

'Harry, I really don't think I'm cut out for marriage. I like you a lot, you know that. But I also like my life just as it is.'

'Now, maybe. Think of the future, Amber. It can get lonely on your own.'

She shook her head. 'I'm sorry, Harry. I'm not the right one for you. I hope you find someone who appreciates you as you deserve.'

He smiled ruefully, raised her hand briefly to his lips, and released it. 'I'm sorry, too. That's a very gracious refusal, my dear. I suppose you've had plenty of practice.'

Amber insisted, 'I mean it. It's a lucky woman who gets you, Harry. I'm probably being a fool to myself.' Harry was the safest bet that she was likely to be offered. A pity she couldn't muster any enthusiasm for the idea.

He laughed. 'Well, if you ever change your mind.'

'Yes, but . . .'

'Don't hold my breath?' he suggested drily.

She shook her head again. 'We can still be friends?' He was disappointed, but she didn't think his heart was shattered. She hoped not. Harry was such a gentleman, he would be careful not to show it if it was.

'Of course we're friends, Amber,' he assured her, pushing back his chair. 'Always.'

As she rose to join him, he smiled down at her. 'You're looking anxious,' he said. 'Don't. It's not your fault.'

They walked back to the gallery arm in arm, and he left her in the foyer. 'Thanks for coming, Amber. And don't worry about me, promise?'

She looked up at him. 'I promise.'

He smiled. 'Mind if I claim a goodbye kiss?'

Amber lifted her face. She could hardly refuse him that.

He did it properly, folding her into his arms and kissing her mouth, then patted her cheek and said, 'See you in New York. Don't let it be too long, OK?'

'OK.' She stood smiling after him a little sadly as he disappeared into the passing crowd, and then turned to go into the open doors of the gallery...

To find Joel leaning on the door-jamb with folded arms, and a decidedly nasty look on his face.

She started almost guiltily, and then, annoyed with herself, squared her shoulders and swept past him with her chin definitely leading. 'Hello, Joel,' she said. 'I wasn't expecting you. Harry said you were looking for a studio.'

He followed her towards her office, scarcely glancing at the few people staring at the pictures. She opened the office door, and went round the desk to drop her bag in the lower drawer. When she straightened, Joel was standing in the doorway. She said, 'Does that mean you've decided to stay?'

He came into the room and closed the door. 'Harry told *me* he was going to buy presents for his family,' he said. 'I didn't see him carrying any parcels.'

Amber shrugged. 'Did you find a studio?' she asked.

He was looking at her as though he didn't hear, as though he was fighting some fierce inward battle with himself.

'Joel?' she prompted. 'Have you found a place to work?'

'Yes. Where did you go with Harry?'

'Little Athens.' When he looked blank, she said, 'It's a restaurant. They do a nice lunch. Where's the studio? Is it what you want?'

'I wouldn't have taken it if it wasn't.' What she could only think of as a look of cunning entered his face. 'Want to come and see it?'

'No, thanks. Not now. I'm late as it is.'

He scowled then. 'Yeah. A long lunch, wasn't it?'

He sounded so accusing that her hackles immediately rose. 'I didn't notice the time passing,' she said.

'Hmmph. Enjoying yourself too much, were you?'

'That's right. I told you the food was good.' She gave him a limpid smile. 'Now, if you'll excuse me, I've got work to do.'

She pulled out her chair and sat down, opening another drawer to take out a cashbook and pen. When Joel didn't move, she looked up at him with an air of impatient enquiry, the pen poised in her hand.

'Why was he kissing you?' Joel asked.

She felt the colour creep into her cheeks. 'I don't think that's any of your business, do you?'

She should have known better than to ask a rhetorical question of Joel. He seemed to consider it quite carefully, behind the deepening scowl. 'OK,' he finally conceded. 'But you weren't pushing *him* away.'

'If he'd started pawing at me, I probably would have,' Amber answered, at her most crisp. 'Now, as I said, I have——'

Joel came away from the door so fast that she flinched.

'Pawing!' He leaned over and plucked the pen out of her hand, throwing it down on the desk, then flattened his palms on the wood.

Amber's head jerked up, the fright in her eyes quickly replaced by a cold anger. 'Don't you touch me!'

He stared at her. 'And don't you dare me!' he said, his eyes meeting hers unswervingly.

There was a light tap on the door, and as Dinah opened it Joel straightened and Amber tore her gaze from his. She saw that her hands had curled into tight fists on the desk, and deliberately relaxed them.

'Oh, you're back,' Dinah said, and, noting Joel's presence, 'Sorry, I didn't realise——'

She glanced curiously at them, and Joel moved towards the door. 'It's OK. I was just leaving.'

When he had gone, Dinah asked, 'Are you all right? You look flushed.'

'I hurried back,' Amber said. 'Thought you might be needing me.'

'Oh, it's not been too busy, but there is one query. I've written it all down, and the phone number to ring. I didn't realise Joel was here. I wouldn't have interrupted.'

'It wasn't important. He was just telling me he's rented a studio.'

'Oh, where?'

'He didn't get around to saying. You know how vague he is. Now, let's have a look at what you've got here.'

He crumpled paper. 'And that you, baby doll,' he said, 'is leaving here tomorrow.'

There was a little tap on the door, and as if on cue, a young woman entered. Amber saw she was much taller than she herself was, and that she wore her hair cut short and close to her head.

CHAPTER SEVEN

AMBER took Harry to the airport. Joel came, too, and when the plane had lifted into the sky he turned to her. 'Coffee?' he asked hopefully.

Amber shook her head. 'I have to go back to work. Dinah's on her own.'

He loped beside her as they walked to the car. 'What about dinner tonight?'

'No, thanks.'

'Got a date?'

'No date.'

'Angry with me?'

She stopped and looked at him. 'Why should I be angry with you?'

He looked back at her solemnly, then grinned. 'No reason. Do you need one?'

She'd never thought of herself as a particularly quick-tempered person. But, she realised, since she'd met him she had spent a good deal of her time being angry with Joel.

Someone jostled him from behind, and he moved closer, hooking an arm about her waist to urge her towards the door. 'Come on, let's get out of this crowd.'

He sat beside her in the car, wrapped in a notable silence until they neared the gallery.

'Can I drop you somewhere?' Amber asked him.

'The gallery will do.' Then he said abruptly, 'When can you start to sit for me?'

'I'm very busy. With your exhibition,' she reminded him pointedly. 'How much time will you need?'

'Hours. One will do to start. Can you come after work today? I'll give you something to eat afterwards.'

She had already turned down dinner with him. But this sounded different. Business rather than a date.

'OK,' she agreed. 'An hour.'

He turned up at closing time, and she said, 'You didn't need to fetch me. You gave me the address.'

'I thought it would be nicer if I called for you. You don't mind, do you?'

'No, but I've got my car.'

'It's OK. I walked.'

It took five minutes in the car, and she parked just down the street from the old sandstone building that had been converted into studio flats. Joel's was on the ground floor. He hadn't yet had time to produce the chaos that had characterised his apartment in New York, but the couch was strewn with clothing and newspapers, and an open suitcase was on the floor in one corner of the living-room. A glassed-in conservatory, bare of plants and with a floor of wide polished boards, opened from the main room and led into a tiny courtyard garden. He had set up an easel in the conservatory, where the light would fall on it. A peacock chair sat facing the easel. There was a bamboo screen across another corner.

'Nice,' she said.

Joel was standing by the easel when she turned from the window. 'All right,' she said. 'What do you want me to do?'

He ran his eyes critically over her cream suit and fawn silk blouse. 'Get those clothes off for a start,' he told her, and jerked his head towards the screen. 'Behind there——'

Amber exploded. 'I'll do no such thing! I said you could paint me—but I never agreed to let you do a nude study. I am not taking my clothes off, and if that's what you had in mind you should have spelled it out!'

'Amber——'

'No! You want a nude model, I know several good ones. Professionals.'

'Don't be offended,' Joel said patiently. 'I just want——'

'I said no. Forget it.' She made to walk towards the door.

He intercepted her, a hand about her arm. 'Come here, you idiot woman!' He drew her firmly after him towards the screen.

'Don't call me names! And if you think you can force me to——'

'Shut up,' he said, 'and look.'

He had taken her behind the screen. There was a straight-backed chair there, and hanging on the back of the screen a gown. Full-length, with long sleeves and a high collar. It looked old, made of silk taffeta that had been washed many times until it lost its original stiffness. The material was printed with some kind of exotic design, reminiscent of Paisley, but with a vaguely Eastern flavour. The dominant colour had been a brilliant pink, but it had faded to a kind of sunset glow, and the pattern included turquoise and blue and emerald green—peacock colours. The front fastened with a line of black silk frogs.

'I want you to wear that,' Joel said. 'Is it modest enough for you?'

Amber clenched her teeth. 'You might have explained.'

'I was about to,' he said, 'when you flew at me.'

'Where did you find this?' She fingered the material.

'A second-hand shop. Put it on before the light goes altogether.'

She put it on, and when she came out, feeling faintly self-conscious, he positioned her on the chair, which was now almost side-on to the easel, with her head turned to face him. She could see that she had ceased to be a woman for him. His gaze was abstracted, his hands impersonal, placing her as though she were a store mannequin, even tilting her chin to the angle he wanted. Only when he touched her hair, brushing the strands away from her ear to fall on her shoulders, for a moment she saw a hint of awareness as his eyes met hers.

Then he went to the easel and silently began sketching in pencil, with swift, sure lines, squinting at her, then making sweeping strokes as he stood back from the easel, or moving closer to fill in some fine detail. After a time he grunted, tore off the paper he was working on and, scowling fiercely, began again.

He let her rest briefly once, and changed her position a couple of times, but she still found posing arduous. He talked little, and she dared not initiate a conversation because she didn't want to break his concentration.

After an hour he said, 'OK, that'll do for today.'

He was frowning at what he had done, and she said, 'Aren't you pleased with it?'

'Mm?' He looked up abstractedly. 'I don't know yet.'

'I'll get changed.'

He left the easel and stood more or less in her way. 'I wish you wouldn't.'

'You said we'd finished.'

'I promised I'd feed you. We could eat here, I thought. Aren't you comfortable in that?'

Firmly, Amber shook her head. 'I prefer my own clothes.'

He stepped aside. 'OK. I have eggs, ham, salad. Or we could go out.'

'What you have sounds fine.' She disappeared behind the screen.

She left her jacket off, because the room was quite warm. Finding the kitchen, she hesitated in the doorway. 'Can I help?'

'Sit down,' he suggested, indicating the two chairs flanking a table in the corner.

He made quite a creditable meal, and she thanked him for it as he served cheese and thick slices of French bread to follow.

'You sound surprised,' he said. 'Thought I subsisted on bread and tins, did you?'

'You look far too healthy for that,' she admitted, although something of the sort, she realised, had been her unconscious assumption.

He leaned back in his chair, popping a cube of cheese into his mouth. When he had chewed and swallowed it, he said, 'You really don't think much of me, do you?'

'As an artist, I think you're brilliant.'

'And as a man?' He leaned across the table, his eyes challenging hers.

Amber's back pressed against her chair. 'I'd prefer not to have this conversation, Joel.'

'But we are having it.'

'You are.'

He got up, and she stiffened, willing herself not to cower. But he only stood looking at her thoughtfully.

'Want coffee?' he asked at last, and she nodded gratefully.

After he had handed it to her he resumed his seat and stared broodingly into his cup while she almost finished hers.

He said suddenly, 'Harry's not the man for you.'

'That's my decision,' Amber retorted tartly.

'And?' He looked up, his eyes searching.

'And what?'

'And,' he said impatiently, 'have you made one? A decision. About Harry.'

'How many times,' Amber asked, 'have I told you to mind your own business?'

'I've lost count. It would save you the trouble if you just answered the question.'

It would probably be simpler, she reflected. 'You don't have any right to ask it,' she said. 'Thank you for the meal.' She pushed away her cup. 'Now it's time I went home. Unless you want help with the dishes?'

'Not with the dishes, no.' He got up and handed her jacket to her. 'Can you come tomorrow? And at the weekend.'

'If you like.' The sooner they got it over with, the better.

'One more thing,' he said, as she stood at the door. His hands went to her hair, and Amber felt her heart give an odd little thump. But he wasn't attempting to pull her closer. Instead, he was lifting her hair with his fingers, back from her cheeks and up, studying the effect.

'Joel——'

'Yes,' he said, but it wasn't an answer, except to his own inward query. 'Have you got a comb or something? I mean the kind that will hold your hair up?'

'No, I haven't. Joel——'

'Get one.'

'*Joel*!'

He looked down at her with mild surprise. His hands were still in her hair. 'What's the matter?'

'I'm not a *prop*!' she said tartly. 'And I don't *want* a comb for my hair.'

'All right,' he said mildly. 'I'll find one, then. That'd be better anyway. I can get what I want.'

'What you want me to wear.'

'That's right.' He seemed very happy with the idea.

Amber quietly steamed all the way home.

She left work early the next afternoon, asking Dinah to finish up.

'No problem,' Dinah said. 'Going somewhere nice?'

'I'm going to get my portrait done,' Amber replied gloomily. 'If Joel ever gets his sketches right. So far I think he's thrown away four.'

Joel had found a comb. She had to admit it was beautiful, a long-toothed tortoiseshell comb, delicately designed.

Resignedly she put her hair up according to his instructions and seated herself in the chair, while he brooded over her with the expression she had come to know that excluded everything except his work. He leaned down and gently drew out one long tendril to lie against her cheek, then withdrew to the easel.

He worked for a time in his customary silence, then suddenly asked her, 'Heard from Harry?'

'No. Have you?'

He grunted. 'Didn't expect to. Did you?'

'Not particularly.' For a moment his hand paused, his eyes questioning her. 'He'll be in touch.'

Joel nodded. His eyes returned to the paper in front of him.

When he said, 'Take a break,' Amber stretched the stiffness from her limbs and wandered to the window, looking out at the courtyard. It was weedy at the edges and moss grew in the cracks of the paving. Plants spilled from a couple of pots, and ivy had taken over the brick walls.

'Your garden needs tidying,' she observed idly.

'I like it,' Joel said, coming to stand beside her. 'It looks pleasantly neglected.'

'It looks neglected, all right.'

'You don't approve.'

Amber shrugged and turned away. 'It's your garden.'

He said, 'Stay there a minute.' Returning to the easel, he sketched her just as she was, then standing by the chair. Then he sat her in the chair again. He worked with fierce concentration, but each time he tore off a page of the sketch block he seemed less than pleased with what he had done. Sometimes he went on sketching when he told her to stop posing. Some drawings he put aside, some he screwed up and threw down on the bare floor.

He said, 'Are you hungry?'

She had been posing for two hours. 'I guess I am. I'll make a meal, if you like. If you have anything to make it with.'

'Fruit, cheese, bread and salami.'

He was sprawled in the peacock chair when she came to tell him it was ready.

She thought he was asleep, but when she approached the chair he looked up at her and said without any preamble, 'You don't want him, do you?'

'What?'

'Harry. I needn't have bothered.'

'Needn't have bothered with what?'

'Keeping him out of your way. Carting him off to Ayers Rock. He didn't even appreciate it. "It's big," he said. "Now can we go back to Sydney?"'

Amber said, 'Harry's a city dweller. He'd be a fish out of water.'

Joel shook his head. 'Guess he really wanted to get back to you.'

Amber said carefully, 'Do I understand that you deliberately tried to keep him and me from being alone together?'

'You didn't twig to it?' He looked inordinately pleased with himself.

Harry had hinted at something of the sort, but she had refused to take him seriously. 'Why on earth would you do that?' she demanded.

'Don't play dumb,' Joel said. 'You know perfectly well why.'

She felt herself flushing. She had tried to avoid this, even in her own mind. But Joel was determined to make her face it. She shrugged uneasily. 'Let's eat,' she said, and began to move away.

He leapt up from the chair and was instantly beside her.

'Why do you keep running away?'

'I'm not running away,' she answered calmly. 'I need some food.'

He gripped her arm, bringing her to a halt. 'You know what I mean.' And as she veered, trying to escape him, he grabbed her other arm and gave her a little shake. 'You do!'

Amber forced herself to meet his eyes, and to make hers as cold as she could. 'All right. I don't suppose I'm the first woman you've wanted, nor likely to be the last. And I don't see that it entitles you to adopt a dog-in-the-manger attitude!'

'All's fair,' he said. 'And Harry isn't the man for you.'

'And you think you are?' Her lip curled. 'Don't make me laugh!'

He said, 'I don't want to make you *laugh*.' And then he pulled her into his arms and kissed her.

His mouth was warm and firm, and his arm slipped about her and kept her held against him. Her hands pushed at his shoulders, but there was no avoiding the pressure of his lips, persistently persuading hers to part.

A shiver of pleasure ran through her, and one of her hands closed on a fold of his shirt, clinging. When he raised his head and looked questioningly into her eyes, she gazed back in bewilderment.

He smiled and feathered a finger across her lips. '*That's* what I wanted.' He placed his big hands carefully on each side of her face and tilted it, his eyes on her mouth again.

Amber tugged at his wrists. 'No,' she said breathlessly. 'Don't, Joel.'

He didn't move. His eyes sharpened. 'Why not? You're not going to tell me you don't like it.'

'I just—this isn't—it's not for me.'

His eyes laughed at her. 'Why not?' he repeated. 'You thinking of going into a convent?'

'It's not a joke!' she said. 'Let me go!'

His hands dropped. 'OK. I've let you go. Now tell me what the problem is.'

'A woman is entitled to say no.'

'Sure. That doesn't explain why *you're* saying no to *me*.'

'You're not that irresistible, you know!'

'Only to you.' He grinned at her. 'Go on, admit it.'

'Huh! You'd be lucky.'

'But you didn't resist, did you? At least, not so's you'd notice.'

'You might have noticed,' she retorted, 'if you bothered to think about anyone's feelings but your own.'

'Watch your tongue, lady,' he said. 'I could make you take that back in about one minute flat.'

'Don't you even think about it!' Amber rose to the threat like a fish to a fly, her whole body instantly geared to resistance, every nerve taut and quivering.

'And I warned you before about daring me!' Joel said.

They glared at each other across two feet of space. Amber felt the blood racing in her veins, bringing a flush to her cheeks. Joel seemed bigger than ever, and he was flushed a little, too. His mouth was grim, his eyes dark.

'I'm not daring you,' Amber said irritably. 'But I won't be bullied.'

'I don't bully you!'

'What would you call it, then? You *made* me——'

'I didn't make you do anything you didn't want to do.'

'Oh, that's typical! You know what I want better than I do, I suppose?'

Belligerently, he said, 'Well, maybe I do, at that!'

Amber lifted her eyes to the ceiling. 'Spare me!'

Suddenly he laughed. 'OK,' he agreed, reverting to his usual infuriatingly amiable mood. 'If you want me to slow down, I will. But you got me here, Amber. I told you I didn't want to come, and now that I have I'm not backing off just because you've had an attack of nerves.'

It took her breath away. 'I know you didn't want to come to Sydney,' she said, 'but if you think I'm going to pay you for it by——'

'Stop right there!' Joel ordered loudly.

She did, because the amiability had totally vanished. He looked dangerous.

Amber swallowed. 'I think I'd better go.'

'Yes,' he said. 'You're damn right, you'd better.'

Her head lifted, she stalked past him. She heard him walking behind her, and clamped down an instinctive urge to run. When he reached round her to open the door, she moved away from him so quickly that her back came up against the wall with a small thud.

Joel frowned at her heavily. 'You're not *frightened* of me, are you?'

Amber's lips curled in a smile of splendid derision, and she forced herself to meet his astonished gaze. 'Don't be stupid.'

But she was aware of the speculative narrowing of his eyes as he watched her walk to her car and get in.

On Saturday afternoon he seemed to be making an effort to be impersonal. He asked her to pin up her hair with the tortoiseshell comb, and didn't even touch her when she took up her pose in the big chair, but as he worked his expression became more and more morose, and finally he flung down the pencil he was using, staring at the sketching block in obvious frustration.

'Isn't it going well?' Amber asked unnecessarily.

He looked up at her, still scowling. 'I wish you'd——'

'What can I do?' she asked.

'Nothing you'd be willing to do,' he said. 'At least, nothing you're going to admit that you're willing to do.'

She looked away from him, remotely. 'If that's all you can think about——'

'I'm not talking about sex,' he said cuttingly. 'Can't *you* think about anything else?'

'*Me*?' Amber gasped, incensed.

'Yes, you,' he said rudely. 'Every time I come near, you give me that look that says, "Don't dare touch me, you carnal animal!" Well, frankly, lady, I'm not that interested——'

'I'm glad to hear it!'

'I'm not that interested,' he repeated deliberately, 'in trying to make love to a woman who goes all coy whenever I start to get close to her.'

'Coy!' Amber stood up. 'Just because I don't re- ciprocate when you decide you're bored enough to grab the nearest female, even one you don't particu- larly like——'

'There you go again!' he roared. 'If that isn't coy, then I don't know what is!'

'I have no idea what you're talking about.'

'Huh!'

'Well, I don't!'

'You know damn well I like you!' he accused her. 'I *told* you I do! If I didn't, why the hell should I want to kiss you?'

'If you did, why the hell didn't you want to come to Sydney?' she demanded. 'That seemed a clear enough indication that you'd changed your mind about liking me.'

He stared at her. 'You can't believe that. Are you that insecure?' he asked wonderingly. 'I didn't want to come because I was really attracted to you, but you acted as if I was one step up from the dirt under your feet. It may come as a surprise to you, but I'm not that keen on rejection. I didn't feel like putting myself on the line for another one. And you had something going with Harry, anyway. So what was the point?'

'I didn't have anything going with Harry—not seriously, and anyway——'

'You didn't tell me that,' he pointed out. 'You wouldn't tell me anything about it. So what was I supposed to think?'

'Nothing. It really didn't matter to me what you thought. I'm sorry,' she tacked on as an afterthought.

He looked disbelieving, and just a tiny bit smug. 'So why were you so keen for me to come here?'

Amber stiffened. 'Don't flatter yourself. I wanted you here for the opening.'

'And longer. A few months, you said.'

'So that you could produce more paintings—for me to sell. I told you, I thought being back here might stimulate you.'

He gave her an odd little smile. 'And that's the only reason?'

'I'm sorry if you misunderstood. I suppose,' she said fairly, 'that you've got accustomed to having women chasing after you. But in my case you were mistaken. I want your art, not you. And I really thought that you'd—lost interest in me. Except, maybe, as a sort of challenge to your ego.'

'And you like giving out challenges, don't you?' He wasn't smiling now.

'I'm not! I'm just trying to analyse your behaviour.' She guessed he'd thought it might be fun to make her succumb to him, after all. Not only did he not like rejection, he probably wasn't accustomed to it either.

'While you're about it, try to analyse that kiss you gave me the other night,' he advised sarcastically.

'I didn't give you a kiss. It was taken.'

'Oh, yeah?' His eyes gleamed. 'Well, don't tell me you didn't enjoy it.'

She had no intention of telling him anything. 'You obviously have plenty of experience,' she said. 'It isn't necessarily a recommendation.'

He blinked at her, and then grinned. 'Words at ten paces, is it?' he suggested. 'Fire away, but I warn you, if I run out of ammunition I just might get physical.'

Amber's fists clenched. Her voice shaking, she said, 'Yes, that's a typical male reaction. I might have known you'd be no different.'

Surprised, he came towards her, frowning. Amber stood her ground, and was surprised in her turn when he took one of her hands and gently prised open her fingers.

Her nails had made faint marks on the skin of her palm. He cast her a concerned, puzzled look. 'There's no need for that,' he said chidingly, and lifted her hand, touching his lips to the marks before she snatched it away from him.

'And there's no need for *that*,' she said curtly.

Joel smiled. 'Let's go out. I can't work any more today. We could do with a break, both of us.'

She should say she'd go home. But instead she said, 'Where do you want to go?'

'Out of the city,' he suggested. 'I want trees.'

They found trees. Tall eucalypts with peeling grey bark revealing the smooth white tenderness of the trunks beneath, and long papery leaves twisting in the breeze. Ferns gathered about the feet of the trees, and a red-earth path led uphill to a point where they could look down at the city and the harbour in the distance.

Joel hooked a casual arm about Amber's shoulder as they stood admiring the view, breathing hard because the climb had been steep.

'The bush is drying out already,' Amber said. 'I hope this summer isn't going to be too dry.'

'Fires?' Joel guessed at the faint worry in her voice.

'Mm. Last year was bad. Some people lost their homes.'

'I read about it.' He looked down as she turned to him. 'I get papers from home sometimes.'

'You have no family here, do you?' She moved away, and his arm dropped.

Joel shook his head. 'I was an only child. My parents are dead.'

She looked at him curiously. The statement told her nothing. She had seen it half a dozen times in articles written about him; obviously it was something he trotted out for each interview. But, hearing it now, she sensed something behind the bare facts.

'Were you very young?' she asked.

'No.'

She said, almost unwillingly, trying to imagine him as a child, 'What were they like?'

'Good people.' He stopped abruptly. 'Very good people. Missionaries. They worked overseas, in various trouble spots. Eventually trouble caught up with them. They died together in a terrorist ambush. It wasn't even meant for them. They just got caught in the crossfire.'

'You didn't go with them, to these trouble spots?'

'Oh, no. I spent my childhood here in Australia, on a farm in Gippsland. When I was six months old they left me with my grandparents, because it was safer, and because caring for a small child would hinder their work. The work of God.'

'They must have been very dedicated. Did you mind?'

'Sometimes. My mother used to ask me that. "Do you mind?" she'd say, and then launch into an explanation of how important their work was, and how we all must make sacrifices so that God's word could be heard all over the world, and bring peace to the nations.'

'She felt that was more important than being with her child.' Amber wasn't judging. Her voice was non-committal.

'My father did, anyway, and their church was traditional in its ideas. Wives obeyed their husbands.'

Their church, Amber noted. Not his. So he had not followed their beliefs.

'Sometimes she cried,' Joel remembered. 'And I'd tell her no, I didn't mind. I told her I was happy.'

Amber turned to look at him, and he said almost defensively, 'It was true, most of the time. It had always been that way. So I didn't miss them. Until my grandmother died.'

'How old were you then?'

'Twelve. My grandfather became very feeble and forgetful after that. He had to go into a nursing home. I wanted to be with my parents then, but they said it was too dangerous, and I should finish my education. I was sent to a church boarding-school. It was a good school. Then, when I was at university, they were killed. I'd never got to know them.'

'That's what's in your pastels,' she said. 'It must have hurt, doing them.' It had not struck her the first time she saw them, although she had experienced the poignancy which each one conveyed, strangely at odds with Joel's public personality, if not as starkly so as his other work. It wasn't until she had seen the pastels hung in the gallery that the overwhelming theme of all of them had emerged unmistakably. Alienation, loneliness, separation. Each picture featured landscape and people, but the people seemed overwhelmed by distance, the vast distances of the landscape, and the smaller but visible distances between each of them. Husbands and wives, parents and children, black people and white. Always he had depicted them turning away from each other, or staring at each other across some empty space which one sensed they would never bridge.

Joel said, 'Art isn't worth doing unless it hurts.'

CHAPTER EIGHT

As AMBER drove them home, Joel asked, 'Are your parents still alive?'

Amber shook her head.

Joel waited. When she said nothing more, he asked, 'Any brothers or sisters?'

'Two brothers. One is in England. His wife sends a card every Christmas. The other moved to New Zealand a couple of years ago. They're both a lot older than me. We were never close.'

'I always thought, if I hadn't been the only one, it would have been different.'

'Not necessarily,' Amber advised drily.

Joel slanted her a glance. 'You weren't happy as a child, either.'

She said with mockery, 'Are we trading poor-little-me stories? I don't remember much about my childhood. I was probably as happy or unhappy as anyone else.'

Plain, thin and shy, hopeless at games, and unmercifully teased because of her red hair, she'd felt an outsider all through her childhood. Playmates had not been encouraged, and she was ashamed to invite them home, anyway. At her house there was no mother to dispense cold drinks and biscuits, and she was painfully aware that, in spite of her efforts at cleaning and tidying, which her stepfather and brothers treated with amused and occasionally irritated tolerance, there hung about the place an air of uncaring squalor.

As a teenager she had suffered agonies because her pale skin didn't allow her to acquire a fashionable tan like other girls, and her breasts hadn't developed as early as theirs. At the same time, their giggling conversations and naïve sexuality embarrassed her, and they thought she was a snob. She'd thought of herself as a freak.

With adulthood had come the realisation that the girls she had so envied had also suffered adolescent agonies over their acne, or their extra weight, or even their precocious, over-abundant figures. Some of them now used colour rinses to make their hair look like hers and dieted fiercely to emulate her natural slenderness.

'How did you get into the art business?' Joel asked her.

'I was quite good at art when I was at school. That and mathematics. At one time I thought I might take it up as a career.'

'Why didn't you?'

'Because I don't have enough talent. I learned that at art school. I worked in galleries off and on in between other jobs, and when a small one came on the market I bought it.'

'You make it sound simple.'

He couldn't have guessed at how much she had left out. The fierce determination to be dependent on nobody, the years of slaving at two jobs, sometimes three, saving every cent she could spare, the difficulty of finding a bank that would back her with a loan. 'I was lucky. The owner was willing to leave some money in the business.' But, even when she had the gallery, it wasn't easy getting the art world to accept that at twenty-four she knew what she was doing and was no soft touch. She'd developed a reputation for being a hard-nosed businesswoman. Astonishingly, she had discovered that some people claimed to be afraid of her.

'More than lucky, I'll bet,' Joel guessed. 'You worked hard for what you have.'

She nodded, oddly pleased that he'd recognised the fact. 'That, too.'

'Is that why you've forgotten how to play?' he asked.

Amber's face tightened, her guard instantly going up. 'Just because I don't want to play with *you*,' she said, 'you needn't assume I don't know how.'

She knew he was studying her, but studiously she kept her eyes on the road. Then he folded his arms and settled back in his seat. 'You can't resist, can you?' he said.

She risked a quick glance at him. 'Resist what?'

'Throwing out a challenge.'

'It wasn't a challenge,' she protested crossly. 'It was a statement.'

'Huh!'

'Oh, do——' Shut up, she wanted to say. But that would give him the satisfaction of knowing he had needled her.

He had turned his head to look at her again. He waited. 'What would you like me to do, Amber?' he asked finally, his voice coaxing and suggestive.

'Grow up!' she snapped.

Joel burst out laughing.

When he asked her to stop so he could buy some chicken and chips for them to eat back at the studio, she demurred. 'It's getting late.'

'Poof!' he scoffed. 'It's not late at all. Have you got a date for tonight or something?'

She didn't, but before she had decided whether to invent one he added resignedly, 'I know, it's none of my business. The thing is, I'd like to do a bit more work on the painting. If you can spare the time.'

She looked at him, suspicious of his formal, almost humble tone.

He said, 'I think it will go better now. Well, after we've had something to eat. And wine. I'll get a bottle of wine. Relax you—us.'

'I'm quite relaxed, thank you.'

He looked as though he was about to argue, or laugh again, or maybe both. But he didn't. 'Me, then,' he said. 'It will relax me. I'll work better.'

'What about the light?'

He sighed. 'I never knew such an obstructive woman. Don't worry about the light. It'll be fine.'

They ate the boxed chicken in the conservatory-studio. Joel spread a cloth on the floor and placed wine glasses on it with the bottle, dropped a couple of large cushions and threw down some paper towels.

'Don't you own a table?' Amber asked.

'Yes, but this is better. Do something for me.'

Amber lifted her eyes from a doubtful contemplation of the meal, and asked warily, 'What?'

'Put on the gown—the one I bought for you.'

The one he wanted to paint her in, she amended in her own mind. His way of putting it sounded too intimate for her taste.

'Supposing I get grease on it?'

'I won't paint in the stains,' he promised. 'Look, I'm trying to establish a mood, OK? I want to paint a woman, not a business machine.'

Amber stiffened, and he closed his eyes, then opened them again and said, 'Sorry. I didn't mean that. Just—please, Amber. I want to get it right.'

She shrugged, and walked across the room to the screen. She put on the gown. It had begun to feel familiar. The silky material was cool and soft next to her skin. She removed the two plain clasps with which she confined her hair these days and swept it up into the loose knot that Joel liked, securing it with the tortoiseshell comb. The fit of the gown was slightly loose, skimming her breasts, waist and hips. But when she moved, the fabric, thinned with age, tended to cling to her legs. She unconsciously walked a little taller, a little more slowly to accommodate that fact, and the length of the skirt.

When she emerged Joel had opened the wine and poured some into the glasses. He looked up in the act of putting down the bottle, and for a moment didn't move. Then he gestured for her to sit on one of the cushions. The light was dim. Critically, she squinted up at the single bulb overhead. 'You'll never be able to work in this.'

'Never mind. I've got some lamps. I can bring a couple in here if I need them.'

He picked up the striped box and offered it to her. Amber took a chicken wing, and bit into it.

Joel kept pouring wine unobtrusively into her glass. He talked as they ate, lazily and amusingly, telling her stories about New York, about other painters, about his own early days in the international art world. When the chicken was all eaten, and the bottle emptied, she found herself sitting against the peacock chair, her legs curled to one side under the splendour of the faded gown, one arm casually resting on the seat, her other hand holding a half-full wine glass, while Joel sprawled near by, his elbow on a cushion, gently twirling his own glass in his fingers, still talking.

He fell silent rather suddenly, watching her as she raised her glass and sipped at it.

'That's it,' he said softly, as she lowered it again, and looked enquiringly at him. 'Don't move!'

He got to his feet, and as she straightened to shift her arm from the chair seat he repeated sharply, 'I said, don't move! Just stay right where you are.'

As she looked at him, startled and a little resentful, he stopped in the act of turning away from her, to come back and bend swiftly, tipping her chin infinitesimally with a finger, to drop a light kiss on her mouth. 'Please,' he breathed. 'Don't lose the mood, Amber.'

She tried not to. The wine helped a bit. She was feeling pleasantly rested and just the faintest bit muzzy. Deliberately she pushed aside her resentment. The sooner they got this over with, the better.

He fetched an adjustable lamp and set it where it cast a light on his easel, and some on her as well. He frowned at the paper on it, and Amber asked, 'Can I finish my wine?'

'Mm?' He looked up. 'Oh, yes. Fine.'

'Thank you.' She sipped it slowly. Yes, she was quite relaxed now. Joel knew how to achieve that in a model.

For no reason, her mind reverted to his studio in New York, and the girl—what was her name?—Trudi.

She had certainly been relaxed, draped on Joel's sofa. Very much at home.

Joel said, 'What are you scowling at?'

'I'm not scowling.' She smoothed the unconscious lines on her brow.

'You were. That's better. A bit.'

He worked in silence for a while. Amber tried to think of something else. After a time, her arm began to ache, and her back. She said, 'I need to move.'

'Mm,' Joel muttered, his pencil moving over the paper with long, slashing strokes.

'Joel! I'm cramping up!'

He looked up. 'Oh, sorry. All right, take a break.'

'Thank you,' she said grumpily. She lowered her arm, rubbing at her shoulder, and shifted the skirt of the gown so she could get up without tripping on it. Joel came over to help her, lifting her easily to her feet.

She moved a hand to the faint crick in her neck, and Joel turned her so that she stood with her back to him, and then his hands were firm on her shoulders and nape, massaging the tension away.

'Thank you,' she said after only moments, stepping away from him. 'You're good at that.'

'I could show you some more things I'm good at if you'd let me.' She looked scornful, and he added, 'What have I done this time?'

'Nothing.' Maybe there hadn't been a double meaning there at all.

He grinned suddenly. 'You've got a nasty suspicious mind, Amber.'

'I've no idea what you mean. Have you done enough for today?'

'I suppose you're tired,' he admitted reluctantly.

She shrugged. 'I'm not a professional model.'

'OK. Come again tomorrow?'

'I suppose so. I'll help you clear this up.' The remains of their meal were on the floor. She bent and picked up the bottle and his glass.

'You needn't,' he said.

'I don't want to find them still here tomorrow,' she told him drily.

He laughed, and scooped up the table-cloth. 'I would have removed them——'

'Oh, yes?'

'Before you arrived.'

She gave him a look of extreme doubt, and he followed her to the kitchen, protesting in aggrieved tones, 'I'm not a total pig.'

Amber didn't reply, rinsing the glasses and placing them on the sink counter. She rinsed the bottle, too, and the two cups and a plate that she found already in the sink.

Joel opened a rubbish bin and tipped the remains of the food into it, shaking the cloth before bundling it up and dumping it on the small table, among a pile of newly washed linen and clothes, a dish of fresh fruit and a scattering of opened mail. No wonder they hadn't eaten at the table, Amber thought. There wasn't room!

'Women,' Joel complained, 'are all the same. Ask them to sit for you, and they can't resist cleaning up.'

Amber looked about for a tea-towel. A striped edge peeking from the heap of washing on the table seemed promising, and she moved towards it hopefully. 'Part of this mess is mine,' she said. 'And I don't want to confront it in the morning.' She grasped the striped edge, and flicked the tea-towel out of the pile. 'I have no intention of making a habit of cleaning up after you.'

'Thinking of staying the night, are you?' he asked conversationally.

Remembering what she had just said, she answered tartly, 'Certainly not. You asked me to come tomorrow, didn't you?'

He leaned against the counter and watched her meticulously dry the glasses. When she picked up a plate he said, 'That's not your mess.'

Amber glanced down and replaced the plate on the drainer, putting down the tea-towel with it. 'You're right,' she agreed. 'Do it yourself. I'm going to get changed.'

'I wish you wouldn't,' Joel said, reaching out a hand and stopping her as she made to pass him. His hand curled firmly about her arm, and he came away from his lounging pose and moved closer to her, his eyes alight. 'I wish you'd stay.'

Afterwards, she blamed the wine for the fact that she didn't immediately pull away. Instead, she let him draw her to him, heard him murmur, 'I like you in this,' as his hands slid over the fabric that covered her arms, closed on her shoulders and tugged her against his chest. His eyes seemed to have hypnotised her, until his lids lowered as he looked at her mouth, and then his head came down and her own eyes instinctively closed under the sweet shock of his kiss.

He took his time over it, savouring the taste of her mouth, enjoying the softness of it, exploring its shape, and then experimenting with his tongue until she opened her lips and allowed him to find his way inside. She felt his hands slide round to her back and down to her waist, felt her head fall back under the weight and the depth of his kiss, her body arching forward into his to compensate. Her hands were about his neck, her fingers buried in the surprising silkiness of his hair. Their mouths were locked in a silent, secret delight. She knew nothing, felt nothing but the delicate sensations he was evoking with his lips and his tongue, her whole being centred on the kiss, on Joel. His hands were on her hips, tracing the shape of the bones through the thin fabric. Then they stroked down, and slowly up again. One arm wrapped about her waist, and the other hand continued upwards, the thumb finding each of her ribs on the way, until his palm rested on her breast, and Amber sighed with pleasure.

He withdrew his tongue from her mouth, and turned his head a little, firmly licking the moistness of the kiss from her upper lip, then her lower one. She shuddered, her eyes tightly shut, her head still tipped back. The texture of his tongue was exquisite. More. She wanted more.

The warm hand on her breast shifted, and she felt him undo the top fastening of the gown, exposing the small hollow at the base of her throat. And then his tongue...yes, his tongue, the tip of it darting into the hollow, and his lips enclosing it.

His fingers fumbled with the next fastening, and the next, skimmed across her skin, just touching the upper curves of her breasts. Then they slipped to her neck, and the hand about her waist, holding her so closely, swept upwards, until he held her face in his hands, and her eyes slowly opened to the blaze of his.

'Amber,' he said, his voice slurred with passion. 'Come to bed with me.'

'Joel...' Her voice was low, surprised. 'Joel...' She should say, I don't do that. She should say, No, Joel. She should...

'Please, Amber?' He moved one hand, gently stroking a strand of hair back from her cheek, her temple, and then he lowered his mouth to the pulsebeat there, and mumbled again, 'Please, Amber.'

She had never wanted anything so much in all her life. He had lifted his head again, waiting for her answer. She looked at his mouth and wondered why she had never noticed how beautiful it was, its firmness and softness.

He tipped her head a little further, impatiently, and made her look at his eyes, the pupils enlarged, drugged-seeming, but with the glitter of desire in the dark irises.

Maybe hers were the same, because as she looked at him his expression changed, became confident, demanding. 'Say yes,' he whispered to her, but with a new air of command. 'Say yes, Amber.'

For a moment longer she gazed back at him, trying to understand what had happened to her, knowing it made no sense, knowing she didn't want it to. 'Yes,' she said at last, and, on a long, unsteady breath, 'Yes, Joel!'

She wakened slowly. First she was aware of light on her closed eyelids. It must be morning. Then she was aware of a strangeness in the atmosphere, before she opened her eyes.

She saw the taffeta gown lying on the floor, its colours ablaze in the morning sun, before she saw Joel, sitting on a kitchen chair in the corner of the room, dressed in a pair of jeans with no shirt, his head bent over a large sketching block, his pencil busy. He glanced up, said, 'Hello,' in the most casual way imaginable, and kept on drawing.

Amber became conscious that she was lying in Joel's bed, naked, and that the sheet barely came to her waist. She reached for it, and he glanced up again and said, 'Don't move.'

Amber sat up, fully awake. 'Joel!' she said sharply, as he looked up in exasperation. 'Stop that!'

'A minute,' he muttered, bending his head again. 'I told you not to move.'

'And I told you to stop!' Amber said furiously. Bounding off the bed, she crossed swiftly to the corner and snatched the sketch pad away, turning from him to rip off the page and discard the pad on the ground.

He stood up, trying to take the page from her. But she had torn it once across before he even reached her, and as his arms came round her, trying to rescue it, she tore it again.

She turned to him, his arms loosely about her, and screwed the pieces into a clumsy ball. He grabbed at her wrists, and she dropped the pieces, pulled away from him strongly and said with clenched teeth, 'Don't you *ever* do that to me!'

He stared at the ruined pieces of paper with a wounded expression. 'It wasn't for public consumption, you know. I wouldn't have shown it, if you didn't want me to.'

'I didn't want you to *do* it!' she said. 'How *dare* you invade my privacy like that?'

He looked quite stricken as he raised his eyes from the ruined paper to her face. 'I'm sorry. I didn't think of it like that. It was supposed to be a gift.' He watched as she gathered up the crumpled gown and held it in front of her. His face changed then, became harder. 'Most women——'

As Amber's head jerked up, her eyes meeting his, he flushed. 'I mean——'

'I can guess what you mean,' she said witheringly. 'I'm sure most of them are suitably grateful for your...expert attentions, and the pay-off in a genuine original Matheson afterwards.'

His lips clamped together murderously, and for an instant she wondered how she had ever thought of them as soft. And yet they had been, last night...

She clutched the gown more tightly in her hands as he took a step towards her. Attack being the best defence, she shot at him, 'How many women have one of your grateful gifts hanging in their bedroom?'

He gave an angry bark of laughter. 'Do you expect me to answer that?'

'No,' she said. He had probably lost count. 'I don't give a hoot,' she added coldly.

'Oh, no?' he drawled. He was standing right in front of her now. 'Then why are you acting like a jealous shrew?'

Behind his anger lurked triumphant laughter, and she saw it with a sick, sinking feeling in her stomach. If she had not needed both hands to hold on to the long gown and preserve some illusion of modesty, she would have hit him. Trying to calm herself, she said steadily, 'I'm not jealous. I just feel... cheapened... and it's my own fault.'

'Cheapened!'

'I shouldn't have drunk so much wine.' She tried for dignity, with a wry smile. 'It must have been more potent than I realised.'

Joel stared at her, his eyes hostile. 'Only the wine?'

Amber swallowed, and forced herself to meet his gaze. He had been a wonderful, tenderly demanding lover, finding in her a depth of passion that she had not thought herself capable of. 'You, too, of course, Joel,' she soothed, mocking him. 'You're very...skilful.'

'Why,' he said slowly, 'does that sound like an insult?'

Amber managed a smile, innocent and bewildered. 'Insult? But all I said——'

'I know what you said!' He looked baffled, almost hurt. 'What's the matter, Amber?' he asked, and reached for her.

She backed away. 'Nothing. I don't like post-coital discussions much. Do you mind if we skip it?'

'What, and go on as if it never happened?' he demanded.

'Yes, exactly. And understand one thing, Joel. I have no intention of it ever happening again.'

That rocked him back on his heels for an instant. But then he thrust his chin forward, and said, 'Oh, you don't, huh?'

Amber firmed her lips and shook her head.

'You've got a nerve!' he said softly. 'Standing there, like *that*——' his eyes ran over her, his lips curling at the inadequate concealment of the gown '—and telling me that!'

Amber felt a *frisson* of fear. Her eyes widened.

'What the hell do you think I am?' Joel asked. 'A bloody teddy bear?'

This is Joel, she reminded herself. *Joel*. He wouldn't hurt a fly. I think...

She said, 'You're not an animal.'

'No,' he said. 'Lucky for you.' He was very angry, but he hadn't moved any closer. She didn't much like the way he was watching her.

Amber shifted her shoulders uncomfortably. 'Look, I'd like to have a shower. Do me a favour and go and get my clothes from the other room, would you?'

He looked at her coldly and said, 'No.'

She felt a flush of anger rise to her cheeks. How petty could he be? she thought.

And then he said carelessly, 'Have your shower. But put that on again...' he nodded towards the garment in her hands '...and come into the studio. I haven't finished with you yet.'

Then he turned his back on her and walked out of the room.

Resentfully, she complied. Emerging from the bathroom, she smelled toast and coffee, and when she entered the conservatory Joel was standing looking out at the garden, with a piece of toast in one hand and a steaming pottery mug in the other. Here the breakfast smells were overwhelmed by an even stronger aroma. She saw that he had been mixing paints, and had a stack of brushes ready for use. The sketching block had been replaced by a piece of hardboard.

He turned at her entrance. 'Want something to eat?'

'Just coffee, thanks.'

She fixed her hair while he fetched it. She had rescued the tortoiseshell comb from the bedroom floor where Joel had dropped it last night. He had stood behind her, his lips on the smooth skin of her nape, a hand splayed on her midriff, inside the loosened gown, holding her snugly against him. And it was only after he'd eased the gown off her shoulders, and smoothed its way down her arms with his big, warm hands, that he'd removed the comb, and let her hair fall against her pale skin, and clutched it gently in his hands to turn her face up to his kisses. And when she twisted to nestle into his arms, he had swept the gown down over her hips and let it slither around her feet. And then, without lifting his mouth from hers, taken her the few steps to the bed.

When he returned she was seated in the peacock chair. She took the coffee from him in silence.

He swung away from her, and waited for her to finish. When she did, he swooped and took the cup from her, and, with her wrist in a firm grip, lifted her from the chair. 'The way you were yesterday,' he said. 'The same pose, please.'

She glanced at him and saw that his expression was quite impersonal. She did what he asked, trying to adopt exactly the same position.

But he said, 'No,' and moved her arm, her head. 'Relax,' he grunted. 'Shall I fetch the wine?'

'No.' She made a conscious effort. It was difficult. 'I did have a glass in my hand yesterday, though.'

He went to the kitchen and brought one back, filled with fruit juice. 'OK?'

Faintly chilled by his remote courtesy, she took it from him. 'Thank you.'

He gave her an odd sort of smile, and walked over to his easel, picked up a brush and began working with a quiet, contained savagery. He had the last sketches that he had done on the table beside him, but he hardly glanced at them, only looking at her now and then with a fierce, cold concentration.

Amber felt her back begin to stiffen. She wriggled her shoulders a tiny bit, glanced at Joel and saw him scowling at the board in front of him. She settled back into her pose.

Her arm had pins and needles. She flexed the fingers surreptitiously, and Joel said, 'Keep still.'

She got thirsty, and sipped at the orange juice when he wasn't looking. Her legs had gone to sleep. The rest of her was in some kind of trance.

'All right.' Joel threw the brush into a jar of liquid. 'That'll do for now.'

Amber downed the rest of the juice, and got stiffly to her feet. Her feet were cramped, and her back was on fire. Her neck hurt and her head was developing a dull ache.

Joel, watching her cautiously straighten up, asked, 'What's the matter?'

'I've only been sitting there for hours,' she pointed out, 'getting yelled at every time I moved!'

'I didn't yell at you,' he said with perfect, if irritating truth. 'You should have told me if you were uncomfortable.'

She knew she should have. She wasn't even sure what had stopped her. 'I want to get this finished,' she said. 'I do have other things to do with my time.'

'I know that. I want to get it finished, too. But I can't do any more today.'

'May I see it?'

'When it's finished,' he said implacably, standing in front of her as though afraid she would try to peek.

Amber shrugged. 'Well, then, I may as well go home.'

'Are you always as cool as this,' he asked, 'after——?'

Amber met his eyes, her brows delicately raised. 'I told you, I don't go in for discussion.'

She didn't go in for one-night stands either—or affairs of any sort, but there was no need for her to let him know that he was—special. She started towards the screen with a hidden fear that he might follow her.

But he didn't. When she came out he was standing by the door, and he watched her broodingly as she crossed the floor and made to pass him.

As he didn't seem to be going to say anything, she paused and said, 'Will you need me again?'

He gave her a wolfish grin. Annoyed with herself, she added, 'To sit for you?'

'Yes.'

She said, 'You've made so many sketches, I thought——'

'I can't do it from them!' he said. 'I need you— I'll have to work from life, on this one.'

'It's taking a lot of my time,' she told him.

'And mine.'

'It was your idea!'

'And you're hating every minute, aren't you?'

'You knew I didn't want to do it.'

'Is that why you're holding out on me? Why you won't give anything to it?'

'I've given you hours!' Amber reminded him. 'I've done every damn thing you told me to! What more do you want, for heaven's sake?'

'I want you to open up,' he said. 'Let me get behind that smooth armour of yours. I hoped you'd get used to me drawing you and begin to relax, let me find the real you inside. What are you frightened of, Amber? What are you afraid I might see?'

'I'm not frightened of anything,' she said flatly. 'You're imagining things, just because I didn't like you taking advantage.'

'Taking advantage!'

'Yes. You can't just draw people without their knowledge and consent. Haven't you ever heard of model releases?'

'You told me I could paint you. Not willingly, but I do have your consent!'

'Not to what you just tried to do!'

Joel looked perplexed as well as angry. 'I made a mistake, didn't I?' he said at last. 'I thought that this morning you'd be different. But you've clammed up on me again, shut yourself in tighter than ever. I should have painted you right there in the bed last night, after we made love, before you had time to find your shell again and crawl into it.'

CHAPTER NINE

AMBER felt sick. She should have known—she had known—how single-minded Joel was about his painting. How often, she wondered, did he take his models to bed to get the effect that he wanted? She should have realised. And it was no comfort that this time it hadn't worked as he'd hoped.

She said, 'I'm sorry you didn't get what you were after. I'm very busy this week, but I may be able to come in for an hour or two on Wednesday again, late afternoon, if that's any good.'

He looked disgruntled. 'Can't I see you before then?'

'I really don't think I can fit——'

'For God's sake, Amber——' He grabbed at her arms as though he intended to shake her.

'Let me *go*, Joel!' Her voice was a whiplash, her eyes ablaze.

He did let go, abruptly. 'What the hell is the matter with you? I wasn't going to *attack* you!'

'Just don't touch me, OK?'

'You didn't mind being touched last night!' he reminded her. 'I couldn't touch you enough then!'

'That was——'

'You practically begged me to,' he went on ruthlessly. ' "Yes, Joel, touch me there, and there and—oh, yes, Joel, there! And *please*, there!" '

'Shut up!' She backed from him, flushing painfully. 'Stop it!' she ordered hoarsely. 'Just stop it, do you hear?'

'I don't *understand* you, woman!' he roared in frustration. 'Anyone would think it had never happened!'

'I wish it hadn't!' she assured him passionately. 'I wish to God it never had!'

And she walked determinedly to the door, slamming it behind her in his bewildered face.

Monday afternoon, she was working in her office when Dinah put her head around the door and said, 'Joel wants to see you.'

She was about to tell Dinah to put him off, she was busy, but he had already walked in, with a brief word of thanks to the assistant, accompanied by one of his charm-the-birds-from-the-trees smiles.

'Yes?' she said, as he closed the door firmly behind him. 'Is there a problem? I'm sure Dinah could help——'

'Dinah can't help,' he said. 'This is not to do with selling paintings. I want to talk to you, Amber.'

She looked pointedly at the paperwork spread over her desk. 'I don't have a lot of time.'

'Dinner,' he suggested. 'You can't work all night.'

She looked up, about to phrase a polite, firm refusal, but she knew that dog-with-the-bone look of his. He wasn't going to let go. She sighed. 'All right, dinner. We are talking about a restaurant?' she added pointedly.

He grinned with relief. 'A restaurant,' he assured her. 'No more chicken and chips on the floor.'

That wasn't what worried her. A public place, she hoped, would make it difficult for him to become too personal, and would certainly preclude a physical confrontation.

She picked up her pen, waiting for him to leave. Joel eyed her speculatively, then gave a short laugh and said, 'I'll call for you here when the gallery closes.'

She freshened up before he arrived, and combed her hair carefully back, smoothing it into its clasps. Joel ran his eyes rather resignedly over her under-stated cream suit but said nothing about it. He looked as though he'd made an effort to be presentable himself. His aqua-coloured shirt seemed almost new, and he wore dark blue trousers with it, and a decent pair of casual shoes.

'I've been told there's a good Italian restaurant near here,' he said. 'Feel like Italian?' Amber said she didn't mind. She had eaten at this one before, and she agreed with whoever had told Joel about it.

She ordered a fettucini with a creamy cheese sauce, and Joel tucked into a plate of ravioli. It wasn't until they were drinking cappuccino topped with cream and cinnamon that he sat back in his chair, staring at her thoughtfully, and said quietly, 'You know I want to make love to you again.'

Amber's glance flickered. 'Even famous artists can't have everything they want.'

He leaned over suddenly and placed a large hand on hers before she could draw back. 'Amber—did I kid myself the other night? I thought you enjoyed yourself. Or were you faking it, at the end?'

Without looking at him, she shook her head. There had been no need to fake anything. 'You were great,' she said, her voice light. 'Did I forget to thank you properly?'

'There's nothing to *thank* me for!'

You can say that again, she agreed silently. 'Why spoil a perfect experience by trying to repeat it?' she asked.

'Perfect?' He searched her face.

Amber lifted a shoulder. 'Well—almost.'

'Almost? So why not try for absolutely? What would make it perfect?'

You not having an ulterior motive, for a start, she thought. That would help. Aloud, she said, 'Oh, Joel. You don't expect me to give you a detailed criticism of your technique, do you?'

He was frowning. His eyes cooled and narrowed and his voice altered. 'Why not?' he asked. 'Tell me how you'd really like it, Amber. Next time I'll try for top marks.'

She stiffened at his tone more than the words. He was being deliberately insulting. 'I told you,' she said, 'there isn't going to be a next time.'

His hand had tightened on hers, and she winced, trying to pull away. He looked down, then released her, watching her snatch her hand back, rubbing it briefly with the fingers of the other.

'Did I hurt you?' he asked gruffly.

'Don't know your own strength, do you?'

'Sorry. I just wanted——'

'Yes, we know what you want, don't we?' Amber said with deadly sweetness.

'All right.' He leaned further across the table, holding her eyes. 'Now tell me what *you* want. Really.'

Amber hesitated. Her lips parted, then closed. Finally she said, 'I want you to leave me alone, Joel.'

'Then what was that all about, the other night?' he demanded.

'It was a momentary impulse—a brief fling, if you like! I don't want to be hounded and harassed just because we shared a few hours of pleasure. It was nice, it's over. Don't spoil it.'

'I'd hate to spoil it,' he said with an edge of sarcasm.

'Good.' She was crisp and cool. 'Then let's leave it at that, shall we? Are you getting the bill, or shall I?'

'I am, of course,' he growled. 'I invited you, didn't I?'

'Yes, and thank you. It was——'

'Don't tell me,' he said wearily. 'Nice!'

On Wednesday, as promised, she came to the studio and took up her pose again.

'What have you done to your hair this time?' he asked as soon as he opened the door to her.

It was long enough now to twist into a french pleat. She thought it looked neat and businesslike.

'*You* wanted it long,' she pointed out. 'And I can't have it floating round my face all the time.'

'Why?'

'You mean, why not? Because it gets in the way. And I can't help it if you don't happen to like it.'

'I didn't say I don't like it.'

Perhaps he was learning tact. Or did he actually like it? He was looking at it pensively, as though trying to make up his mind.

Amber moved away. 'I'll go and change.'

Joel worked in morose silence, but meticulously remembered now and then to offer her the chance to stretch her limbs.

'How many more sittings?' she asked.

'One or two should do it,' he said.

After he allowed her to change into her own clothes, he asked, 'Come again at the weekend?'

She hesitated. 'Yes, all right. You can finish it then, can't you?'

'Should do. Can't wait, can you?' he asked wryly.

'You know how I feel about it.' She picked up her bag and went towards the door.

'Yeah,' he jeered softly. 'Scared.'

Amber swung to face him. 'Don't be ridiculous! It's just time-consuming and rather pointless, that's all. I'm sure you could find more rewarding subjects to paint.'

Joel shook his head. 'Nope. You're scared. Like those people you read about in *National Geographic* who think their soul is being stolen from them when you take their picture. You think I'm after your soul, don't you?'

Something in his expression prompted an answer that must have come from deep within her subconscious. 'Aren't you?'

He tipped his head to one side, considering. 'Not to steal it. Just to... show it to you, maybe.'

'No. You want to show it to the world.'

'Is that what frightens you?'

'I'm not an artist, Joel. I'm not accustomed to baring my soul.' Artists like Joel were risk-takers, exposing their rawest emotions to the criticism of anyone who cared to look at their work. She could never do that; it was one of the reasons she would never have made it as an artist herself.

He came closer to her, holding out his hands, and without thought she put hers into them. His clasp felt strangely comforting. 'I won't show it to anyone else,' he promised, 'without your permission. OK?'

She swallowed. 'Thank you. But I can't expect that of you. If it's any good, of course you must show it.'

'You'd let me?'

She pulled her hands from his. 'You don't need my permission. That wasn't in our bargain, was it?'

'Still,' he said, 'the offer stands.'

When he finally put down his brushes late the following Sunday and said quietly, 'That's it,' Amber didn't even ask to see the painting.

She got up slowly, feeling oddly empty. 'I'll get changed, then,' she told him. Her voice sounded thin.

Joel looked up. His eyes looked bleary, and his stance was loose with exhaustion. 'Wait,' he said. 'We should celebrate.'

'I don't think——' Amber began warily.

'I do. Come on. I've got some sparkling wine in the fridge. I saved it specially.'

'Have you really finished?'

He glanced at the easel. 'I've got some things to do on the foreground and stuff. But your part's done.'

She was glad of that, she told herself, not sure why she felt suddenly deflated.

He took her hand. 'Come on.'

She let him lead her to the kitchen, and meekly carried two glasses into the living-room while he opened the bottle. When he had poured for them both, he lifted his glass to her wordlessly and then sank down beside her on the second-hand sofa, sweeping aside the assorted junk that had accumulated on it. He wore a battered pair of jeans and faded, stained T-shirt, and smelled of paint and sweat. He sat back with an air of weary contentment, legs apart, and tipped back his head with a long sigh, then turned to glint a smile at her.

Amber felt a stirring of sexual excitement. Trying to hide it, she unobtrusively shifted an inch or two further away from him as she lifted her glass to her lips, taking a leisurely, cool sip.

'You don't have to do that,' he said. 'I'm too tired, anyway, to leap on you.'

Amber thought of pretending she didn't know what he meant, and gave up, slanting an embarrassed smile in his direction instead. 'Sorry,' she said. And then, on impulse, 'I'll make you dinner, if you like.'

'You must be tired, too.' He flexed his shoulder muscles as though they ached.

'Not like you,' she said. 'I could do with a bit of moving around, after all that sitting still. What have you got in the kitchen besides wine?'

He grinned across at her. 'What else would I need? Dunno. Milk, cheese, eggs, some bread, a bit of some kind of wurst, I think. And a few tins.'

'I'll think of something.'

'Not yet.' He dropped a hand on hers, holding her fingers in a warm, friendly clasp. 'Just sit a while,' he suggested.

He closed his eyes, and she wondered if he had drifted into sleep, but then he lifted his glass again, drank some wine, and opened his eyes to give her another, rather blurry smile. 'Going to stay with me, tonight?' he enquired hopefully.

'No.' Amber removed her hand. 'I'm going to cook you dinner, and then go home. Anyway, you just said you're in no fit state for—what you have in mind.'

'How do you know what I have in mind?' he asked.
'And you're not going to make dinner unless you're
eating with me. At least you can stay that long.'

Amber stood up. 'I'll go and investigate your
fridge.'

She found a cook-and-serve all-purpose deep dish
and made a soufflé which she served with thin-sliced
bread and butter and heated rounds of the tasty
sausage, with tinned anchovies and sprigs of parsley
from the overgrown garden as garnish.

Joel had stirred himself to have a shower and change
while she cooked, and emerged less bleary. His eyes
brightened considerably when he meandered into the
kitchen at her call and watched her set the soufflé
down on the table, which she had cleared of clutter.

When they had eaten it all, he said, 'Thank you,
Amber. Where did you learn to cook?'

'My mother.' Amber was gathering up plates.

'Was she like you?' he asked.

'No. I got my colouring from my father, but I don't
remember him.'

'You must have been very young when he died.'

'I was when he walked out on my mother.'

'Oh? She had to bring you and your brothers up
alone, then?'

Amber answered reluctantly, 'No. My stepfather
moved in.' She put the dishes into the sink, clattering
the knives and forks on top.

'Straight away?'

'No. Pretty soon after, I think.'

As she looked about for the detergent and found
it at the end of the bench, Joel asked, 'How did you
get on with him?'

She had her back to him, squirting liquid on to the dishes, turning on the taps. 'I used to think he was the moon and stars rolled into one.'

'So, is he the one who died? Or your natural father?'

'My natural father was killed in an industrial accident a few years after he left us. That's when my mother and stepfather made it legal.'

'And your stepfather?' Joel had both forearms on the table, his hands loosely clasped as he watched her.

Suddenly she turned to face him. 'As far as I know he's alive and well somewhere,' she said. 'I've no idea where, OK? What else would you like to know?'

Joel stood up. 'Why you're so touchy about it, for a start,' he said. 'Did he desert you after your mother died?'

'No, he didn't! After the boys left he looked after me until I was old enough to live on my own. He's married again now. I don't see him any more.'

'Why?'

'Oh, for God's sake! I just don't!' She threw a plate on to the counter so hard that it skidded right off on to the floor and smashed.

She looked blankly at the pieces. Joel stared at her, then bent slowly and began gathering them up.

'I'm sorry,' Amber said stiffly. 'That was careless of me. I'll replace it.'

'Don't be silly. It's only a plate.' He placed the shards on a corner of the bench. 'I didn't mean to upset you.' He looked at her rather carefully.

'I wasn't upset.' He moved his head, disbelieving, and she said, 'My hands were slippery.'

'Doesn't your stepfather's new wife like having you visit him?'

Amber raised her eyes to the ceiling. 'You can't leave something once you've latched on, can you? I never wanted to visit them.' She added grimly, 'I did go to see her once.'

'And it wasn't successful.'

Amber gave a dry little laugh. 'You could say that.'

'Were you jealous of her?' Joel asked curiously.

He was unprepared for the abrupt whitening of her face. She closed her eyes, her hands stilled in the soapy water before her. 'No,' she said tonelessly. 'Oh, God, Joel, will you leave it alone?'

He reached for her and pulled her round into his arms. 'I'm sorry,' he said against her hair, and again with his lips moving on her temple, 'I'm sorry.'

She shuddered, and then pushed him away. 'All right, apology accepted!'

He looked irked at that, and she said, 'I know you mean well, but I just don't want to be touched right now.'

He took a deep, visible breath, and moved back so that he leaned on the counter, his arms folded. He looked deceptively indolent. 'Why haven't you changed your clothes?' he asked her.

Amber blinked at the irrelevant query. 'I didn't have time,' she said, looking down at the splendid, faded gown she still wore. 'I forgot.'

'Forgot,' he scoffed softly. 'You like it, don't you? Deep, deep down.'

'I haven't thought about it. It's what you wanted me to wear, so I wore it. I'll go and take it off now.'

She whirled away, the skirt swishing and settling. And Joel said, 'I'll do it, if you like. Like the other night.'

Amber stopped in the doorway, keeping her back to him. She had to fight down a wave of heat, of longing. And of fear. 'No, Joel. Never again.'

He said, 'Never's a long time.'

But he let her go.

A few days later he phoned her at the gallery and said, 'Want to come round and see your portrait?'

She had to still a quickened pulse before she could answer. 'No, thank you.'

'Not the least bit curious?'

'Not really.'

'Frightened?' he accused softly.

'No.' But her temples felt damp and cold, and her hand clutched at the telephone receiver much too hard. She suggested, 'If you're so anxious for me to see it, you can bring it round to the gallery if you like.'

There was a moment's silence. Then he said slowly, 'OK. I'll do that.' And hung up.

She didn't expect him to do so straight away, but it was barely twenty minutes later, when Amber and Dinah were discussing the hanging of a new acquisition, that he strode in with a wrapped parcel.

'Your office?' he said to Amber.

'In a minute.'

He strode off, and Dinah said, 'The picture of you?'

'I suppose so. What do you think of that corner there, under the skylight?'

'Yes, OK. Can I see?'

Maybe she could do with some moral support. 'Come along if you like.' There was hardly anyone in the gallery at the moment.

Joel looked from Amber to Dinah as though the other woman's presence surprised him, but he didn't say anything. The two women stood just inside the door as he stripped off the wrapping and propped the painting on Amber's desk where they could see it. And where he could see her face when she looked at it.

Dinah gave a soft, startled, 'Oh!' and looked quickly, apprehensively at Amber.

Whose face was a frozen mask, giving away nothing.

The first impression of the piece was of colour—vivid colour. He had exaggerated and deepened the peacock blues and greens of the gown's pattern, and made the skirt swirl about her and spread across the bare floor. He had painted her hair a shining copper-red. The tortoiseshell comb reflected its brilliance, and one strand of hair had slipped from it and was curled on her neck almost like a slash in the skin. The chair against which she leaned looked bigger than it had in real life, and seemed to loom behind her, its rounded fan-back echoing the shape of the gown's skirt.

But the figure, and the chair, occupied only the top third of the picture. In the lower corner, diagonally across from the figure, was a large masculine foot in a battered trainer planted squarely on the board floor, with a glimpse of a pair of ragged jeans. And between that intrusive foot and the woman by the chair was a seemingly vast expanse of bare boards. But the man's huge shadow spread across them, almost touching the edge of the peacock robe.

Unwillingly, Amber allowed her eyes to meet the eyes of the painted image of herself. They looked very large and defiantly apprehensive, in a face that was exaggeratedly narrow and pale. The way he had painted her limbs, the set of her head, the slight painted her limbs, the set of her head, the slight elongation of her features, gave her a feline look. She looked like a wary, distrustful cat, feeling threatened and ready to spit and claw in self-defence.

She felt her teeth clench achingly, and a pulse in her temple began to pound. Deliberately she tried to relax. She breathed in, then out and said evenly, 'It's a very good painting.'

Dinah cast her a look of surprise. 'You *like* it?'

I hate it! she wanted to say, passionately. I hate it and I don't think I'll ever forgive him. But she said instead, with a little laugh, 'I'm not sure about that. It may take me a while to make up my mind. But it's very *good*.'

She hadn't looked at Joel. She knew he was still watching her, waiting for her to do so. But she couldn't bring herself to meet his eyes—even though she had known he might do something like this, steeled herself for it. She said, 'We could get a good price for it, if you're offering it to the gallery, Joel.'

'I'm not.' Abruptly, he lowered the painting to the floor, turning it from her. 'Dinah,' he added, 'any chance of a coffee?'

'Yes, of course. Do you want one, Amber?' Dinah asked.

Amber shook her head. She could do with a stiff brandy, she thought. But they didn't keep that.

Dinah left, and Joel leaned back on the desk. Moving away from the door to let Dinah use it had brought Amber closer to him.

He said, his voice oddly harsh, 'Would you really sell it?'

She forced herself to look at him at last. 'Of course. I could get a very nice commission on that.'

'You really work at it, don't you?' he said roughly.

'It's my job. I——'

'Not your job! Being the cold bi—businesswoman.'

Her eyelids flickered. 'Are you complaining? You've done very well out of my business ability. I've sold a lot of work for you.'

'Well, you're not selling this!' he said violently, standing up straight.

Amber lifted a shoulder. 'Of course, if you don't want to put it on the market, that's up to you.'

He said, 'Would you really crucify yourself like that?'

You've already done that, she thought, and looked at him finally, fully, with hatred in her eyes. 'As you just pointed out,' she said coldly, 'I'm first and foremost a businesswoman. Of course I would.'

He stood staring at her for more than a minute, it seemed. He looked quite pale, his mouth drawn straight, and his eyes at first challenging, daring her, then filled with a kind of angry pity that stiffened her spine and lifted her chin as she glared back at him, willing herself to remain calm and strong and not give in to the screaming, hurting little girl inside her.

'All right,' he said finally. 'You do that.'

And he walked out, flinging open the door as he went, passing an astonished Dinah on his way, leaving her with his unwanted cup of coffee in her hand.

Amber drank the coffee instead.

CHAPTER TEN

AMBER couldn't bring herself to hang the painting in the gallery and wait for a buyer. Instead she advertised it privately through her network of regular customers and other gallery owners. And was unsurprised when Harry Gates sent her a fax message to say he had a buyer. He had handled a lot of Joel's work, and must have had his own network of potential buyers. She was relieved that the painting would be going to some unknown collector on the other side of the world. Someone who didn't know her.

She asked Dinah to telephone Joel and let him know about the sale. She hadn't seen him since he had walked out of the gallery, leaving the portrait with her. And didn't want to, she told herself, ignoring the hollow feeling that persisted in making itself felt in her midriff.

Dinah came back from the phone saying, 'I can't get hold of Joel. His number's been disconnected.'

'He probably forgot to pay the bill,' Amber said after a moment. It would be just like him. 'I'll drop round after work and let him know.'

She caught herself humming later in the day as she ticked off the items in a crate of metal sculptures that had arrived for her next showing. And when the clock crept towards five, she kept looking at it, determined not to leave before then. She even made herself wait until it showed five past the hour before saying casually to Dinah, 'Come on, time we locked up and went home.'

When she drew up outside the old house, she had to pause to draw a couple of quick deep breaths. Oddly nervous, she went up the path and rang the old-fashioned bell at the door.

It pealed inside in a strangely empty way, and she felt a slight shiver of foreboding. After ringing again, she left the front door and went around the back of the house, where she could look into the conservatory.

It was empty. There was no easel, no screen, no big chair. Nothing. She could see through the open door of the conservatory into the house itself, and it was obvious that no one lived here any more. The place was deserted.

Feeling numbed, she returned to her car and drove home. Joel had cleared off without a word. Gone out of her life.

She told herself it was just as well. They were no good for each other. She had nothing to give to any man, and he must have recognised that. He was, after all, a very percipient person. Witness his portrait of her.

She shivered. And kept on shivering, unable to stop until she had made herself a hot drink with shaking hands, and crawled into bed.

She sent the cheque she received from Harry to Joel's New York address, and went on with her life as best she could, dragging herself out of bed each morning, and going through the motions of living, breathing, working. Told herself it was ridiculous to let a man affect her this way. They had scarcely known each other, after all. He had probably forgotten all about her by now. Probably was inveigling some other woman into his bed, with or without a promise to paint her. Sketching her lying there after a night of loving, presenting her with the results: a genuine original Matheson to hang on her wall in remembrance of him.

Amber was different. She didn't want to remember. Not at any price.

She made a trip to New Zealand, scouting for new talent, and brought back several paintings and small sculptures, with the promise of more to come.

'Tough trip?' Dinah asked her as they uncrated the pictures. 'I hoped that you'd find a change as good as a rest, but it doesn't seem to have worked.'

'Is that a way of telling me I look a hag?'

'Of course not. But you have been looking tired lately, and I'm sure you've lost weight. You work too hard. Why don't you go home and rest? I can manage these and the customers. It's not busy.'

'Thank you, Dinah, but I'm fine.'

Her assistant looked doubtful, but she knew better than to argue. Amber was the boss, and, although Dinah loved working for her and they got on well, there was an invisible line that she knew she would never cross. She couldn't bring herself to tell Amber that she looked, hauntingly, more and more like the disturbing portrait that Joel Matheson had painted of her.

About six months after Joel had left, Amber flew to New York on one of her regular trips. She had to nerve herself to visit Harry's Apple Gate Gallery. But this time the gallery was crowded with people admiring the work of an up-and-coming young artist having her first major exhibition, and Harry detached himself from a group to greet her and kiss her cheek.

Standing back, he surveyed her warmly. 'Lovely as ever,' he said, 'but Amber, what have you been doing to yourself? You're a wraith! Have a bad flight?'

'The flight was fine,' she said. 'Dinah says I'm overworking.'

'Dinah may be right. Let me look after you while you're here. A drink at my flat, after this is over? Come and meet the painter. You'll like her. And she has a great future.'

She did like the rather shy young woman whose paintings showed a flair and drama entirely lacking in their creator, and she circulated as expected, greeting old acquaintances and finding new ones, and now and then she felt a flutter of some emotion between dread and delight when she caught sight of a dark head in the crowd. But each time she experienced the same sick disappointment when the head turned and she saw the man's face, and it wasn't Joel.

She was glad when Harry appeared at her elbow and said, 'Let's go. I can safely leave now.'

He let them into his apartment and took her coat, switching on lamps as they moved into the large living area.

'What would you like to drink?' he asked her.

'Coffee, please. I've had enough alcohol. What have you acquired since I was last here?' she asked, looking about the room. 'Oh, that's new, isn't it?' She wandered over to admire a large modernist canvas that had replaced a landscape she remembered.

'Like it?' I've bought something else that may interest you, but I hung it in my bedroom. I'll show you later.'

He made the coffee and they drank it while talking in a desultory fashion about various artists and their latest work.

'I could do with some more Mathesons,' Harry said reflectively. 'Do you know where he is, Amber? Has he holed up in Australia somewhere?'

Amber looked at him in astonishment. 'Isn't he here, in New York?'

Harry looked puzzled. 'He came back from Sydney, cleared up a few business matters, left instructions about his payments, and then to all intents and purposes disappeared. There's been none of his work on the market for six months. Not in Australia, either?'

Amber shook her head. Fear sharpened her voice. 'Could something have happened to him?'

'Oh, I don't think so. He obviously had something planned. But I've no idea what it was. And that reminds me,' he said, as he saw her cup was empty, and drained his own, 'come into the bedroom and I'll show you what I promised you, before.'

She should have been prepared, she thought afterwards. But she wasn't. With Harry's hand on her elbow, she entered the room, and swept a cursory glance over the velvet-covered king-size bed and the dark walnut furniture before Harry turned her in the middle of the room so she could see the painting facing the bed.

'There,' he said. 'I think you'll agree that it's not something to be hung in the living-room for all to see. I hope you don't mind my putting it here.'

Why hadn't she guessed that Harry was buying the portrait for himself? She felt sick. Gulping in air, she said, 'It's yours. You're entitled to put it wherever you like, Harry. I . . . I'm glad you like it.'

Get me out of here, her mind screamed. But Harry was talking. 'I'm surprised you let Joel put it on the market,' he was saying. 'He was right, I suppose. I didn't know you as well as I thought. When I saw this, I realised it was true, and yet I'd never guessed at that aspect of your character. I can only admire you both—him for recognising it, and you for allowing such a—an exploration.'

Amber's teeth were gritted. She moved away, towards the door, pulling out of his light hold.

'Amber?' Harry was coming after her when she blundered painfully against the door-frame, knocking her elbow.

'Are you all right?' Harry asked, his arm coming about her waist.

Amber gasped. 'Yes.' She rubbed at her arm. 'Just a bump. It hurts a bit.' The swirling spots before her eyes were growing darker by the second.

He led her back to the living-room. 'Can I get you something? You're awfully pale.'

'I'm always pale, Harry.' She tried to smile at him, unaware of the effect it had, her eyes huge in a white face.

'I'll get some brandy,' Harry said abruptly, and when he brought it insisted that she drink it.

'What a fuss over a little bruise,' she said as she finished it.

He looked at her searchingly. 'Was that what it was? Or the painting? I'm sorry if I've done the wrong thing, Amber. I . . . I have to admit that I bought the portrait partly because I felt—well, I suppose much the same way that a Victorian gentleman might have felt if a woman he cared for had modelled nude, and he found the painting up for sale at a public gallery. Silly of me, I suppose.'

'It wasn't silly,' Amber said. 'It was very sweet of you, Harry. And I appreciate what you did. Really. I—can I please have some more of this brandy?'

He poured her a generous measure, and then another. On top of the moderate amount of wine she had drunk at the exhibition, and after a long international flight, it was probably rather unwise, but Amber was beyond caring. Harry was an old friend, and she was far away from home, and at some time after midnight she began telling him things she never would have in her saner, sober moments. A long time after that, she woke up to find herself lying on Harry's sofa, tucked under a duvet and with a pillow behind her head, while the morning light filtered in through the blinds on the window behind her.

'Got a head?' Harry's voice enquired, as she winced and raised a hand to her temple.

'You could say that,' Amber admitted huskily. 'Did I pass out?'

'Not exactly. You weren't in a fit state to go back to your hotel, though. I'd have given you the bed, only I wasn't sure, after what you said last night, that you'd want to wake up and literally look yourself in the face.'

'You're right, I wouldn't. What *did* I say, last night?' she enquired cautiously.

'Quite a lot. You had a bad time as a kid, didn't you, Amber?'

Amber closed her eyes. 'I'm sorry I inflicted that on you, Harry. Ignore it. It was probably all nonsense, anyway.'

'About your stepfather?'

'I loved my stepfather!'

'Yeah, and he loved you, didn't he?'

Amber swallowed, and forced herself to open her eyes. 'Don't worry about it, Harry,' she advised. 'It was all a long time ago.'

'Mm-hmm.' He sat down beside her. 'Ever seen a psychiatrist, Amber?'

She shook her head. 'We Aussies are not into that kind of thing as much as you are over here. We pretty much sort out our problems ourselves.'

'Or bury them in your subconscious?' Harry guessed.

'That's not such a bad place for them to be,' Amber said.

'If that's where they stay. But sometimes they surface, bust out of there, interfere with what you're trying to do with your life. Stop you from living, even.'

Amber swung her legs to the ground. 'My life is exactly as I wanted to make it, thanks. I'm grateful for the use of your sofa, Harry, and for your concern. Really. But I don't need your advice.'

Harry shrugged and stood up. 'OK. But if ever I can help, Amber, you know I'd like to.'

'Thanks. Can I use your bathroom? And then I'll be on my way.'

When she got back to Sydney there was a message on her answering machine from Dinah. 'Someone has been trying to contact you. I told him when you'd be back, and he said he'd call at the gallery.'

Joel? But wouldn't Dinah have said so? Unless, perhaps, he had asked her not to. No, it wasn't like Joel to play coy games.

'No one I'd seen before,' Dinah told her when Amber turned up at the gallery next morning. 'Thirtyish, fairish, quite good-looking. Big bloke. Nice smile. Bet he knows it, too.'

No, Amber said to herself, her mouth drying. Why would *he* want to see me, after all these years? 'If he comes in again,' she said, 'tell him I'm out, and let me know he's here, if you can, before he leaves.'

But when Ron Winter walked in later that day, Amber was on duty at the desk near the door. There was no avoiding him.

She looked up and there he was, big and bulky, with the familiar baby-blue eyes and the too-well-remembered smile that creased his cheeks into disarming dimples. His hair might be a little further back on his broad forehead, and his waist a little thicker, but he looked hardly older than when he had first smiled at her like that, when she was barely seventeen and fresh from Queensland, new to city life and ripe to fall into the predatory hands of a superficial charmer with the instincts of a piranha.

'Well, hi, there, darling,' he drawled. 'Long time no see.'

'Not long enough for me!' Amber snapped. 'What are you doing here?' Art was hardly an interest of his.

'Looking up an old flame,' he said, still smiling, his eyes sending messages that once would have had her heart dancing a fandango. He moved his gaze over her in a way that sent a cold shiver down her spine, and then took a lightning look about the gallery.

His eyes came back to her. 'Saw your photo in a magazine I picked up at the doctor's. There was a bit about you. Successful businesswoman, gallery owner, travels all over the world buying up expensive art work. I'd never have imagined it.'

She remembered the article. She had been one of several young business and professional women profiled, about a year ago. The magazine must have been very out of date. At the time, the article had brought a slight upsurge in trade.

'Show me around,' Ron said.

'I don't show people round.'

'Not even me?' he wheedled.

'Especially not you!'

The smile stayed. That was the worst thing, she remembered. He had never stopped smiling. Even when, as now, his eyes were filled with fury, with the threat of retribution.

Even when that retribution came. That had been the most horrible part of it. That he enjoyed it so much.

Amber stifled a shiver, and straightened her back. 'You don't frighten me, Ron. You can't hurt me.'

His eyes darted about them, spotting the few people strolling about looking at the gallery's exhibits. Softly, soothingly, he said, 'I don't want to hurt you, darling. You know I wouldn't do anything bad to you.'

If she hadn't felt so sick, she might have laughed. He had put her in hospital for two weeks, before she came to her senses and mustered the strength to leave him. And still she had been too afraid of him to go to the police and have him prosecuted. She had just left the hospital without a forwarding address, hidden herself in the anonymity of Australia's largest city, and hoped he would never find her.

'Remember the good times we had,' he coaxed.

There had been good times, at first. He had been big and handsome, and protective. He'd seemed as gentle as a baby. How deceptive that had been. In a matter of weeks he had charmed her into his bed, and she thought that she was lucky, that this kind, wonderful man was going to take care of her for the rest of her life. She had moved into his rented flat with him and, besotted with love, told him the story of her life.

'I did a lot for you,' he reminded her.

She had thought so, at first. He had certainly awakened her repressed sexuality, and she had been pathetically grateful to find that she was capable of normal responses. Ron had taken all the credit, and she had been only too willing to grant it to him. Later, when sex had too often become a punishment, she had even accepted his twisted rationale for the violence of his so-called lovemaking: that he couldn't help it—she had aroused his jealousy because he loved her so much, and that her inexperience was the only reason she didn't enjoy their 'reconciliations' as much as he did.

'You owe me a lot, baby,' he told her.

'I don't owe you anything,' she said in a low, gritty voice. 'What do you want?'

'I've had a bad run in business lately. Thought you might like to help me out, for old times' sake.'

'No,' she said. 'I wouldn't.'

His smile was set in ice. 'Aw, you don't mean that, darling. A little investment, that's all. You'll get it back.'

She wouldn't count on it, Amber thought. In any case, she wouldn't have given him a red cent, for any reason whatever. 'No.'

He reached across the desk and grabbed at her hand, squeezing it. 'After all we shared,' he said. 'Remember when you used to tell me everything? I mean——' the pressure on her hand increased until she almost cried out '—*everything*, darling. Didn't you?'

She felt the blood drumming in her head. Her hands and feet were cold. She thought she might throw up. 'If you think you can blackmail me,' she said steadily, 'forget it. No one would be in the slightest bit interested, anyway.'

Angrily, he flung her hand away from him. For an instant, even the smile disappeared. Then it came back, wider than ever. His eyes gleamed with spite. 'Oh, I don't know,' he said, looking round at the dozen or so browsers in the gallery, and Dinah appearing from a doorway that led to the rest-rooms. 'These people might be interested, don't you think? Everyone likes a good juicy story.'

He flung back his head and opened his mouth, and Amber said loudly, 'Dinah, will you call the police and ask them to evict this man, please?'

Then she walked across the floor to the door from which Dinah had just emerged, hearing his voice in the background, hoarse with anger, following her. She caught a few of the epithets but mostly it was undifferentiated sound. Vaguely she realised that everyone else in the place seemed paralysed, all heads turned towards Ron, or towards her, except for Dinah, who was hurrying to her office at a run.

Amber entered the ladies' room and shut the door. Dinah found her ten minutes later, huddled on the floor in one of the stalls. She had been violently sick into the bowl, but that was over. She felt cold and clammy and very, very tired. She made no objection when Dinah took charge of closing the gallery early and getting her home.

She didn't even object when Dinah insisted on accompanying her. She handed over her car keys without demur, and, when they arrived at the flat and Dinah let them in, Amber just stood in the middle of the hallway as though she had no idea what to do next.

In the end, Dinah got her into bed and called a doctor.

'Stress,' the doctor said. 'Stress and overwork.' Time off, peace and quiet, and a course of pills were prescribed. Meekly, Amber took whatever she was told to. She accepted Dinah's offer to find a temporary replacement staff member, and put Dinah in charge of the gallery. 'I'll increase your salary,' she promised tiredly.

'Never mind about that. Just get better.'

After a week, she asked Dinah, 'What did Ron say?'

'I didn't hear it all. I was telephoning. But he left before the police arrived.'

'Has he been back?'

'No. What's the matter with him? Is he dangerous?'

'Yes, but probably not in the way you mean. I don't think he's certifiably insane.'

'You know him well?'

'I did, once. I lived with him for nearly two years.'

She had been so stupid. So young and stupid. When he had first hit her, she had been shocked, but he seemed so remorseful that she had forgiven him. And the next time, and the next. When he really beat her, so that she was bruised, she tried to leave, and he had alternated between threats of suicide, and pleading and promises—keeping her in the house by force and wearing her down with words until she didn't know whether she was more afraid for herself or for him. And somehow he had contrived to make her feel guilty, as though all of it were her fault.

It had taken a stay in hospital and the efforts of a doctor and a social worker to make her see straight again and put her life together without him. Without anyone. She wouldn't trust herself to any man after that. Wouldn't trust her judgement of them. Ron had been her saviour, her protector. And in the end she had needed protection from him.

Dinah said, 'The doctor thinks you could do with a holiday. You haven't had one for ages, have you?'

Amber had always said she didn't need holidays. She loved her work, and it entailed quite a lot of travelling, which she enjoyed. But now the idea took hold. Maybe the doctor was right.

'How about New Zealand?' Dinah suggested. 'You said you liked it there.'

She let Dinah book her a flight.

CHAPTER ELEVEN

WHEN the plane winged down to the airport at Mangere, daylight was beginning to fade. Below them, the Manukau harbour was glassy and faintly pink as they banked over it and came into the runway. The lights of Auckland city were just beginning to come on. By the time Amber got to her hotel, darkness had fallen, and although her room had a view of the other harbour flanking the city, the Waitemata, she could see only the lights of other buildings, and some coloured shimmers in the dark water between central Auckland and the suburbs on the North Shore.

She slept through the night and woke with an urge to escape the city and find a place where she could be quiet and free to do as she pleased.

In the hotel lobby a rack full of brochures promised boat trips, coach tours, plane rides, excursions to caves, mountains, ski resorts, the active volcanic area of Rotorua, of course, and several beach resorts. There were places to stay from top hotels run by international chains to farmhouse accommodation offering pony-rides, bush walks and country life.

And there was a new venture not far from Auckland, where a Maori trust had opened what was billed as a 'unique tourist experience' on tribal land recently returned to them after more than a century of alienation. It featured limestone caves, a glowworm grotto, several dozen acres of native bush and a river for canoeing and swimming. There was also a small craft centre where young people learned traditional skills and sold their work. Day visitors were catered for, there was a dormitory and ablutions block for backpackers, and a guest house offering 'superior accommodation', meals included.

'How do I get there?' Amber asked at the hotel's information desk, after digesting the modestly produced leaflet. 'And can you arrange a booking for me?'

It proved to be a good choice. The rambling old house had large, airy bedrooms with high ceilings, a big, comfortable lounge and a dining-room where the half-dozen guests shared meals at a long, polished kauri table. Amber's room was simply furnished and had french doors opening on to a wide veranda where people could sit in wicker chairs and look down a grassy slope to the river. A dinghy and three canoes had been drawn up on the bank.

The staff were friendly and thoughtful. They were hosts rather than employees, and nothing was too much trouble for them to make their guests feel at home. The bouncy young girl who waited at the table expressed concern that Amber had not finished the meal on her plate, and had to be assured that there was nothing wrong with the food, only with Amber's appetite.

'Wait till Saturday night, when we give you a hangi meal,' Pania promised. 'Looks as if you could do with some feeding up,' she added, with a smile that robbed the remark of any offence. 'Have you been to a hangi before?'

Amber shook her head. Her previous visits to New Zealand had all been hurried business trips, most of her time spent in the cities. 'You cook the food in the ground?'

'That's right. You can watch the men put it down in the afternoon, then we eat in the evening. We'll have wild pork. You eat plenty of that, eh? It'll be good for you.'

'I'll try,' Amber promised.

That afternoon she visited the craft centre, and spent over an hour watching young men chiselling out complicated carvings in totara wood, after their own designs which used both traditional and modern elements. Long tables held finished work, and on the walls hung woven articles made by women, some incorporating feathers and shells as well as ancient stylised decorative patterns handed down through the centuries. On a sunny porch outside, an elderly woman was teaching a couple of teenage girls the art of flax-weaving. She beckoned to Amber. 'Come and sit here. You can try it, too.'

Amber's effort resulted in a small, lop-sided basket which she carried off to her room along with a much more professional one she had bought from the shop.

She visited the limestone caves with a guide, and admired the white stalactites and stalagmites, and the blue, winking lights of a small colony of glow-worms. 'This is not as big as Waitomo,' the young man told her. 'Their caves are famous, of course, but we have some good formations here, and it's unspoiled.'

Unspoiled was the word for the whole place, Amber decided. She had never felt so relaxed. Not for years. The landscape was gentle and green, the river flowed smoothly in a dark, eddying peace. She loved walking in the bush—coolly dim, damp-smelling, hung with vines and carpeted with tiny-leaved creepers, and quiet except for occasional bird calls. There were no snakes here, and it was quite safe to sit down on a fallen log among the ferns, or on a humped root protruding from the ground, and contemplate the trees all about, and a glimpse of blue sky showing through their latticed tops.

The hangi was all that Pania had promised. With other guests, Amber watched the men digging a deep hole for the feast, piling round river stones into it and lighting a roaring fire until the stones had heated through. Then huge hunks of the promised wild pig meat were lowered into the oven, and parcels of potatoes, scrubbed purple kumara, pumpkin pieces, sweet corn cobs, whole cabbages and foil-wrapped fish laid on top before the earth was shovelled back over the sacking which protected the food.

Hours later the hangi was opened and the steamed food served to the guests sitting along the veranda or on the ground outside. Pania presented Amber with a high-piled plate and waited for her opinion. 'Delicious,' Amber admitted with some relief. The meat was tender and sweet, the golden-fleshed kumara soft and flavoursome with butter and black pepper, and the other vegetables cooked to perfection. She actually finished the plate, to Pania's obvious satisfaction.

She stayed for another week, and before she left had a long talk with the elder who was in charge of the craft centre. She phoned Dinah afterwards and said, 'I'm coming home. I've an idea for our next special exhibition.'

On the plane, she took one of the magazines the cabin crew offered, and flipped through it . . . and stopped at the arts page in the middle as a name leaped at her. *Joel Matheson*.

'Yes, I saw it,' Dinah told her. 'Interesting, isn't it? Going off to work for famine relief for six months. Of course, it's quite fashionable now, that sort of thing.'

'I don't think Joel did it because it's fashionable,' Amber said, surprised at an urge to leap to his defence. 'He didn't tell anyone where he'd gone.'

'I'm not knocking him for it,' Dinah said. 'I take my hat off to him, and I hope his book of sketches does well for the famine fund. I wish I had some sort of talent I could use to—well, to better the world. What was this idea you were telling me about, for an exhibition?'

'Oh, the place I stayed at has a Maori craft centre attached to it. The work they're doing is great. Carving and weaving, mostly. The women do wonderful fine weaving in wall-hangings and some garments and accessories, and lovely flax baskets called ketes. No, kete,' Amber corrected herself. 'They told me there's no "s" in the Maori language.'

'Sounds good,' Dinah commented. 'We've always had a good response to our Australian Aboriginal art. This would be something a bit different.'

Thrusting the subject of Joel Matheson to the back of her mind, Amber outlined her plans. The elder had been quite keen on the idea, saying he would call a meeting to discuss it, and suggesting that if the project was approved a group of craftspeople and elders would accompany the works to Sydney, and give demonstrations in the gallery.

The white-haired old man with the shrewd brown eyes and measured speech had questioned her closely about how she intended to show and sell the work. She had the feeling that he was assessing her closely, that he wanted to be sure she was the kind of person who could be entrusted with work into which he and the younger artists and craftspeople he taught had put more than just time and energy and skill.

All good artists, Amber felt, put something of their heart and soul into their work, but she sensed here even another dimension. The link between the artist and his people and their history seemed as strong, to this man, as between the individual artist and the work. If she didn't totally understand the concepts the elder tried to convey, at least she could respect them. In the end it seemed enough for him. She felt that she had passed some sort of test.

She had passed another test, too, during her time in New Zealand. One that she had set herself. One that was much harder. She almost convinced herself over the next couple of months that Joel Matheson was an unimportant interlude in her life. She had regained some of her lost weight, and nearly all her energy. She could, she assured herself, live without a man. It was only what she had been doing for years, after all.

Dinah had never mentioned the incident with Ron, and Amber certainly didn't want to resurrect it. He had not appeared again. Apparently the threat of the police had scared him off.

A few days before the Maori exhibition was due to open, Joel strolled into the gallery as though he had never been away.

He gave Dinah a lazy smile and said to Amber, 'Talk?'

She looked at his expectantly raised brows and lingering grin, and said snappishly, 'I haven't time. We've got an exhibition to organise. Dinah, we're going to need more boxes painted, to show off the baskets and smaller carvings. Can you get on to that?'

'Yes, sure.' Dinah gave Joel a dazzling smile, apparently to make up for Amber's offhandedness. 'How are you, Joel?'

Amber said, 'Excuse me,' and walked off with her pencil and notepad in her hands, making for her office. Trust Joel to turn up out of the blue and expect her to drop everything to talk to him, just because he felt like it. She threw the pad and pencil on her desk, ran a hand through the hair she had recently got cut short again, and dropped into her chair, seething with a mass of complicated emotions—anger, despair, and a kind of agonised delight.

The door was thrust open and Joel stood there. 'I can paint,' he said.

'What?' It was so unexpected, she was thrown. She knew he could paint, for heaven's sake!

'Boxes. I'll paint them for you.' He smiled winningly. 'Then you can put Dinah on to something else, and make time for me—later,' he added hastily, as he caught her fulminating look.

'I won't have any free time until after the opening,' she informed him. She knew she was being bitchy, but who did he think he was? What made him think he could walk in and out of her life whenever he felt like it, and expect her to welcome him with open arms each time he turned up?

'OK,' he shrugged. 'So put me to work. I want to help.'

'I don't need your help!'

'Dinah just said——'

'Dinah isn't the boss!'

He tugged the lock of hair over his forehead. 'Yes, boss, I mean, no, boss. Sorry, boss. Shall I lick your boots, boss?'

'Oh, shut up,' she said, an unwilling smile pulling the corners of her mouth upwards. 'What are you doing here, Joel?'

He looked thoughtful. 'I'll tell you when all this rush is over. You're under a strain just now. Dinah says you've been . . . unwell.'

He'd got a hell of a lot of information in a short time. 'I'll have a talk with Dinah,' she said drily.

'Don't blame her. I was pumping.'

'Obviously. I read about your famine sketch book.'

'Got some copies to sell?'

Amber shook her head.

'I have some with me. I'll bring a box in for you. You won't mind, will you? All the proceeds——'

'I know,' she said. 'No, I don't mind. I'd like to help.'

He brought them the following day, and somehow stayed to help, and along with the members of the Maori group, who were busily organising their work, advising and helping on the display, he became almost a fixture.

Amber had invited special clients and contacts in the art world to be present for a formal Maori opening ceremony which the group had suggested, and arranged for Press coverage of the event in order to give them maximum publicity.

A small crowd, Joel among them, watched with interest the women's call of welcome, followed by formal speeches from the men and short songs, all part of ancient rituals. Afterwards, switching easily to English, the elder, with an heirloom feather cloak flung over his shoulders, welcomed everyone again and invited them to look at and buy the art works, the proceeds of which would go towards educating the tribe's young people.

It was while she was being interviewed, along with the elder, by a TV team sent to cover the opening for a weekly arts programme, that she caught a glimpse of a fair head weaving through the crowd towards her, and her voice faltered in mid-sentence. Instinctively, her eyes sought out Joel, and found him standing at the fringe of the crowd, watching her.

He must have read the desperate, wordless message in her gaze. He frowned and started towards her, reaching her side just before Ron thrust in front of the camera crew. The interviewer was still holding the microphone, saying in politely puzzled tones, 'Yes, Miss Wynyard?' when Joel slipped an arm about her waist and murmured,

'What's the matter, Amber?'

The camera operator plucked at Ron's sleeve. 'Excuse me——'

But he ignored the intervention. His baby-blue eyes shifted from Amber to Joel and back again, and he smiled.

Amber watched him as she would have watched a deadly snake, poised and ready to strike.

'We're interviewing,' the TV front man said indignantly, and Ron glanced at him, then at the microphone and cameras. His smile grew wider. Deadlier.

'Is this the new boyfriend, darling?' he purred.
'Does he know—do these people know——' he looked
around, triumphantly '—what kind of whore you are?
Have you told *him*——' he jerked his head towards
Joel '—what you told me, about what you and your
darling daddy used to get up to?'

Amber felt the blood seeping away from her face.
In the sudden, shocked silence, she distinctly heard
the whirring of the camera and knew it was still
running. And she felt the sudden tensing of Joel's
muscles, his quick, violent movement.

'No, Joel!' she said, instinctively grabbing his arm
as he surged past her. 'Don't!'

He stopped, but he was already inches from Ron's
sneering face. His eyes locked on to the other man's
and he said, between his teeth, 'Get the hell out of
here before I bloody *kill* you!'

Ron blinked, but stood his ground, his smile
widening beatifically. 'Try it!'

Joel bunched a fist. Then four burly Maori men
materialised from the crowd and surrounded Ron, one
of them pushing Joel firmly aside. 'Come on, mate,'
Amber heard one of them say in deceptively friendly
fashion. 'Let's go outside, eh?' And then they were
bearing him away, parting the crowd, hustling him
off the premises with quiet, speedy and absolutely implacable force.

The interviewer was looking horribly embarrassed.
He said, 'We'll cut it out of the tape, Miss Wynyard.
This is an arts programme, and we're not filming live,
fortunately.'

She managed to say through white lips, 'Thank
you.'

'I reckon we've got enough from you, anyway. We'll just go and get a few shots of the art works, OK?' He gestured to the camera operator and turned away.

Other people were tactfully drifting off across the gallery. Joel's hand was on her arm. Dinah appeared at her other side.

'Get her a drink,' Joel said. 'In her office.' And he guided Amber towards it while Dinah sped off to do his bidding.

He put her into a chair, and squatted beside her. 'Hold on,' he said.

'I'm not going to faint.' She'd thought she might, for a few minutes. Almost wished she had. A few minutes of oblivion would have been nice.

'Who is he?'

'He was my lover. Years ago.'

'I see. Why didn't you let me hit him?' Joel growled. 'You don't still have feelings for that bastard, do you?'

Amber shook her head. 'You don't know how nasty he can be. He knows how to hit people. You'd have got hurt.'

His hand, which had been resting on hers, tightened. 'Did you?' he asked tautly. 'Get hurt? Physically?'

Amber nodded.

Joel hissed out a word. 'I wish I *had* hit him,' he said.

Dinah came in with a glass of sherry. 'Here,' she said. 'This might buck you up.'

'Thanks.' Amber took a sip. 'You'd better be out there, Dinah. One of us should be circulating among the customers and making sales.'

'Want to talk?' Joel asked quietly as she finished the drink.

'No. Not now.' She tried to smile at him to soften the refusal. 'I really have to go back to work,' she said, and stood up.

'Amber.' He took her shoulders gently in his big hands. 'I wouldn't hurt you. Ever. You know that, don't you?'

'Yes,' she said, looking into his eyes. 'Yes, Joel. I do know.' She raised her head and touched her lips to his, but when he would have drawn her closer and prolonged the contact she drew away. 'I have to go out there.'

'And face them all?'

Amber nodded. It wasn't going to be easy, but the worst had happened, and now she had nothing more to fear.

He looked as though he was going to say, 'Are you sure?' She could see the words hovering on his tongue. Her mouth firmed, her chin going up.

'Every last one of them is on your side,' Joel said at last. 'Remember that.'

She tried to, and she supposed it was true. Some people, she guessed, had left early. Some wouldn't meet her eyes, and others looked at her with pity, embarrassment or barely hidden dismay. Others showed understanding sympathy, and one or two came right out and said, 'That was a right turn-up. You ought to sue the bugger.'

And, 'Don't worry about it, Amber. The guy's obviously a nutter. No one will take any notice of him.'

The leader of the group who had got rid of Ron gave her a grin and rubbed bruised knuckles. 'Didn't want to go,' he told Joel. 'Felt pretty strongly about it, but we persuaded him he'd be better off having a quiet rest at home. Don't worry, he won't be back in a hurry.'

Joel hovered near by all the time, and made sure she had some lunch, and when at last they could close the doors it was Joel who told Dinah to go home, he'd look after Amber.

It had been the longest day of her life. She collected her bag from her office, and mechanically took out the keys. 'I'll drive you home,' Joel said, and she was too tired and spent to argue. He locked the gallery and took the driver's seat of her car, and said, 'Direct me. I've never been to your place.'

Mechanically, she did so. When he stopped, he asked, 'Have you got anything in there to eat?'

'I don't know. I'm not hungry. Thanks for bringing me home. You've been . . . kind.'

He shook his head and said, 'I'm coming with you.'

He looked with brief curiosity at the sparely furnished apartment, the white walls designed to show off her small collection of superb paintings, the stark black leather chairs, white wool rug on a charcoal-grey carpet, and the several Venetian glass pieces arranged on the smoked glass coffee-table.

'Kitchen?' he queried, and she pointed, then went into her bedroom, dropped her bag on the dressing-table, kicked off her shoes and sat down on the bed. The moss-green plush was soft under her restlessly plucking fingers. After a while she lay down and let her head fall on the pillow. She never wanted to move again.

She had her eyes closed but wasn't sleeping when Joel came in and brushed his lips across her cheek. 'Amber?'

Amber opened her eyes.

'Food,' he said. 'Here.'

He had put it on a tray for her. Soup and a salad, and some rounds of a french-bread loaf he must have found in her freezer.

He watched her eat it, and then brought her coffee. 'What about you?' she asked. 'Aren't you hungry?'

'I had mine in the kitchen.'

'This is awfully good of you.'

'No. Amber—I love you.'

She couldn't move. She sat with the coffee and looked down at it, and could hear him breathing, standing beside her with one hand in his pocket, watching her bent head.

He said, 'It's all right if you can't reciprocate. I just want you to know.'

Her hands tightened on the cup, setting the liquid shimmering. 'Joel,' she said. 'I can't—I'm just——'
She swallowed and tried again. 'I find that hard to believe,' she said flatly.

'Why?'

Amber gave a cracked little laugh, and risked a fleeting look at him, finding the predictable, glowering scowl on his face.

'You love me?' she said scornfully. 'And you go off without a word for six months—longer, in fact. And come back expecting to take up where you left off. What sort of love is that?'

The scowl deepened. He suddenly swung away from her, thrusting both hands deep into his pockets, and strode as far as the window and back. 'The frightened sort,' he said. 'But I came back, didn't I?'

'Frightened?' Her eyes widened. 'You?'

'Drink your coffee,' he said. 'It's getting cold.'

'I don't want it now.' She put the cup down on the bedside table. 'What are you talking about?' she demanded.

Joel's shoulders hunched. 'Look, call me a romantic if you like, but all my life I thought that one day I'd meet a woman I could really be close to, share everything with. Someone who wouldn't—distance me from her life, from herself. Who wouldn't—wouldn't want to hold out on me. Who'd let me into her warmth and never shut me out. Want to be with me always, forever. Who'd want the same things from me. And then I met you.'

'I was never like that, Joel,' she said painfully.

'No. You were aloof and prickly and determined to shut me out. You were the opposite of everything I had ever wanted. And you were what I wanted more than anything in the world.'

'I was?' She looked at him with wary disbelief.

He smiled crookedly. 'Yes, damn you. When I thought you and Harry were a couple it was almost a relief, because it let me out. OK, I thought. That was a mistake, let her go. But you wanted me to come to Sydney, wouldn't take no for an answer, and when you said you'd sit for me if I came, though I knew you hated the idea, I figured you had to have a personal stake in it, even if you refused to admit it. It wasn't one-sided after all. You really did want me, under all that prickly defence of yours.'

That was probably true, Amber thought. She had fooled herself, but not Joel.

'So I figured, if you wanted me that much,' Joel said, 'you'd given me the right to get you to admit it.' He drew a deep breath. 'When Harry came, I was worried. But he went away again and it didn't mean a thing to you. I could see that. But then, it took me so long to get through to you! I kept thinking, this isn't going to work, we're no good for each other, but I went on beating my head against the wall, because I couldn't seem to help it. And when we made love it was as if all the barriers had come tumbling down, and you were exactly what I'd been searching for— and then came morning.'

'And I put the barriers back,' Amber admitted, her voice low.

'Yes. I was stunned, but I thought I had a trump card. I thought I'd topple them again when you saw the painting.'

'Because you'd painted what you saw behind the barriers, the scared little girl behind the woman I was trying to be.'

'The brave woman who could face the world with courage in spite of the fear inside her,' he said. 'I thought you'd see then that I understood, that you could trust me, if you trusted no one else. I thought you'd know that you could let down your guard with me, let me be close to you, and that I wouldn't betray you. And when you rejected that chance, when you deliberately hurt us both, insisting on selling the picture, playing the hard-headed businesswoman to the hilt—all I could see for us was a life of me trying to get inside your heart, and you fighting it with every breath.'

He was right, Amber realised bleakly. She had been too afraid to let anyone get that close.

'I ran away,' Joel said, 'to do what I'd thought of several times before—do something real. Something that might have significance, make a difference. I drove trucks in the desert, manned food kitchens, put

up tents, buried the dead. And there were so many...'
He took a deep breath. 'I thought it would make me
see how unimportant my love for you was, in the scale
of world disasters.'

'I... hope it helped,' Amber said.

'It helped. But it didn't stop the hurt. That stays,
whether I'm with you or away from you. I can't escape
from it. However unimportant it is on a cosmic scale—
for me, it matters.'

'Is that why you came back?'

'I came back because I couldn't stay away,' he said
simply. 'I just—want you, Amber. To have and to
hold. Even if it hurts.'

Painfully, Amber said, 'I didn't mean to hurt you,
Joel. I was just lashing out in all directions, because
I was so afraid.'

'To trust me?'

Amber nodded. 'I'm a very untrustful person. You
haven't asked me about—what Ron said.'

He sat down on the bed. 'He meant your stepfather, didn't he? Not your father.'

Amber nodded, looking down, away from him.
'You see——'

'You don't have to tell me.'

'Let me,' she said. 'I—think I need to.'

He reached out and took one of her hands in a warm
grip. 'OK.'

'It wasn't quite true, what he said,' she started hesi-
tantly, her eyes on their clasped hands. 'When my
mother died, the boys were grown. I was younger,
and when they left, Daddy—that's what I called him—
was all I had. And I was all he had. That's what he
said.'

'So, naturally you were close.'

'He was more of a father than my real one. And I'm sure he loved me. I thought he was the only person who ever would. Because I was such an ugly kid——'

'You were never ugly!' Joel exploded. 'It's not possible!'

'Well, I thought I was. I was always teased about my hair, and I was a pasty, skinny child. Daddy—my stepfather—used to tease too, a little. He called me Funnyface, but he said he said it didn't matter to him, because we were special to each other.'

'Did he *encourage* you to think you were ugly, that no one else would ever love you?'

'I suppose he did.'

'And you believed it. That explains a lot. So you were totally dependent on him for any self-esteem you had.'

'Yes. And I was grateful. After all, he wasn't my real father. He could have put me in a home or something, and left me. Even as a child, I knew that.'

'Because he said so?'

'I don't remember. I just knew. But as I grew up there was a difference in the way he looked at me, and touched me. I tried to ignore it, because I loved him and I didn't want to leave home—where could I go?—and also I didn't want to think that anything he did was wrong. If I told him I didn't like it he'd get angry and hurt. And I . . . didn't want to hurt him. I thought I must be warped, even wicked, to think there was anything bad about natural affection. That's what he called it. I was very confused. And innocent in a strange way in spite of—everything. He'd always kept boys away from me, saying I was too young and he wanted to protect me, and when I left, finally, he called me terrible names. He was convinced I'd found a man.'

'It wasn't you who was warped,' Joel said.

'I know. Only, then, I felt unclean.'

His hand on hers tightened.

'When he married again, I got an invitation to the wedding. I thought I should go, heal the breach, perhaps. I don't know. The woman was a divorcee with two young daughters, about eleven and thirteen. I thought about it for weeks, and, for their sake, I tried to warn her. I should have known better. He'd told her I was psychotically jealous about him, and might try to make trouble. She believed him.'

'And you told all this to Ron?' he asked quietly.

Amber closed her eyes. 'Oh, yes. I told him everything. I kept nothing back from Ron. I gave him ... everything of myself. So when I left him, I had nothing left for anyone else.'

Suddenly his hand tugged away from hers. She opened her eyes and saw him stride over to the window, pulling at the curtain with one hand until she thought he would tear it from its rail.

'You're angry with me!' she said.

'I'm trying not to be.' He faced her then, his eyes glittering with it. 'You threw yourself away!' he said. 'On that bastard. Why?'

Amber swung her legs to the floor and stood up. 'For heaven's sake, Joel! I was *seventeen* years old! And I needed someone! What did I know?'

'Yes,' he said with an effort. 'Yes. But—him! How could you?'

'Well, where were *you*?' she cried. 'Bedding down in New York with one of your models, or some teenage Lolita like Trudi?'

'*What*?' Joel was outraged.

'You're all the same!' Amber accused him. 'All of you!'

'Now you listen to me, lady!' he yelled, and strode over to her, so that she backed up against the bed as his face was thrust close to hers, his eyes blazing. 'I'm not like your stepfather, and I'm not like your un-savoury ex-boyfriend! And get this straight! I have not ever made love to Trudi! She's a kid beginning to find out what it means to be a woman, just testing on nice, safe older men like me. And, believe me, she is safe with me! Because I wouldn't dream of touching her, even if her parents weren't good friends of mine. And as for models—you know damn well what kind of paintings I do. How many models do you think I've had? I hardly ever use them! Not even for painting, and certainly not for anything else!'

Amber sat down on the bed, shaking, her hands to her face. 'Oh, Joel! I'm sorry!' she whispered. 'I didn't mean to say such terrible things. You're right. We couldn't have a normal, loving relationship. I *am* warped. I'd just keep hurting you, and fighting you, and you don't deserve that!'

He slipped to the floor in front of her and prised her hands away to hold them again in his. 'Amber, tell me one thing. Do you love me?'

Amber looked away. She didn't have the right to bind him to her. If only she had the strength to say no, to send him away so that in time he might find someone kinder and more straightforward, someone open-hearted and sweet-natured, without all the cruel hang-ups that burdened *her*.

'Amber!' He gave her hands a little shake. 'Do you?'

Her throat hurt. She felt tears gather in her eyes. 'Go away,' she whispered desperately. 'Joel, you have to go away from me.'

'Do you love me?' he insisted.

A tear fell hotly on his hand, and he drew in a breath and his hands moved to her shoulders. 'Say it, Amber. Go on, *say* it!'

Dumbly, hopelessly, she shook her head.

'Dammit, woman!' he groaned, his face assuming a fearsome scowl. 'Will you tell me the truth?' And then he was hauling her into his arms, before he pushed her back on to the bed, his mouth devouring hers in a furious, passionate kiss, his body pinning her down against the lush green spread.

She tried to fight it for all of two seconds but he took absolutely no notice of her shoving against his shoulders. She gave up and wound her arms around his neck instead, and gave as good as she was getting.

Several minutes later he lifted his mouth from hers and said unsteadily, 'Now will you say it?'

Amber sighed. 'I love you—but you shouldn't have made me say it.'

'Why?' he demanded.

'You always say that—"Why?"—like a three-year-old child.'

'I'm not a three-year-old child,' Joel growled. 'And I can prove it to you, if you like.'

She smiled a little sadly and touched his hair with her fingers. 'You'll never get rid of me now, and you'd be far better off with someone nicer, and less mixed up, and softer——'

'Boring,' Joel said. 'I guess we're both a bit mixed up, and there'll be fights and misunderstandings and sparks flying while we sort ourselves out. But I need you, Amber, and when you looked at me this afternoon you sure looked as though you needed me. So I guess we're stuck with each other, huh? We'd better learn to like it.'

'If you're sure that's what you want...' she said doubtfully.

'I know I certainly don't want to be on the other side of the world from you any more. I missed you like hell, your ornery temper and your sharpness, and your stubborn pride. Besides, how many women have hair that Titian would have killed to paint? I knew you'd cut it as soon as I turned my back,' he added darkly.

'I'll grow it again.'

'Will you?' He rubbed his chin against it, grazing her temple. 'Good.'

'You need a shave,' Amber said, running a finger over the faintly visible stubble. She smiled again, less sadly. 'But not as badly as you did the first time I saw you.'

'Shall I go and have one? Have you got a razor?'

Amber shook her head. 'No, don't go away. Not yet.'

He said, 'Do you think you can stand living with me? Because I want to marry you. You know that,' he warned her.

She said, 'You'll leave your socks under the bed, and never do the dishes if you can help it, and ignore me when you're working, except to roar at me if I try to make you eat something——'

'And you'll nag at me to put on a clean shirt every day, and pay the bills and be nice to your customers— I suppose you'll keep the gallery?'

'I suppose. Handy for selling your work. Sounds like an old married couple,' Amber said dreamily.

'Sounds great,' Joel insisted contentedly. 'Doesn't it?' He nuzzled her lips with his, parting them gently. His hand wandered until it lay covering her breast.

'It sounds,' Amber said, a little indistinctly against his inviting, questing mouth, 'like heaven.'

WORDFIND #9

```
M A T H E S O N D C S E R B
A S D F R H E R Y T J K U A
O I J A M A V T C F G H Y R
A S F D C R W E E R T K E R
X R E V G E I U J R H G N I
S E T E R E J I O U C R D E
C B S N E R L O K J A E Y R
N M M T S E W A E X R C S B
A A Z U D F G H J L E U I O
P W E R F G J U I O E O P P
W E Q E E R T Y U I R O L K
M M O R N I N G G R C V B N
Z X C V B N M L K J H G R E
D A P H N E E C L A I R T Y
```

ADVENTURE	JOEL
AMBER	MATHESON
BARRIER	MORNING
CAREER	SECRET
CLAIR	SHARE
DAPHNE	SYDNEY

Look for A YEAR DOWN UNDER Wordfind #10
in October's Harlequin Presents #1595
WINTER OF DREAMS by Susan Napier

WF9

Calloway Corners

In September, Harlequin is proud to bring readers four involving, romantic stories about the Calloway sisters, set in Calloway Corners, Louisiana. Written by four of Harlequin's most popular and award-winning authors, you'll be enchanted by these sisters and the men they love!

MARIAH by Sandra Canfield
JO by Tracy Hughes
TESS by Katherine Burton
EDEN by Penny Richards

As an added bonus, you can enter a sweepstakes contest to win a trip to Calloway Corners, and meet all four authors. Watch for details in all Calloway Corners books in September.

CAL93

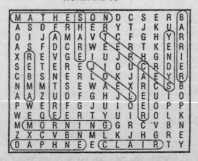